Joshua,

Thank you for s... is,
j... with me!

THE WOLF QUEEN

CERECE RENNIE MURPHY

Cover Illustration: Len Yan
Paperback Cover Design: Deranged Doctor
Hardback (Special Edition) Cover Design: Jesse Hayes, Hayes Design Studios
Map Illustration: Winter-Herbert
Print Design & Typesetting: Ampersand Book Interiors

Author Photo: Kea Taylor, Imagine Photography

LionSky
PUBLISHING

WWW.LIONSKYPUBLISHING.COM

Dedication

To my ancestors,
who sacrificed everything so that I could be.

AND TO ARYEH AND SKYE:

May you feel the greatness within you, always.
Mommy & Daddy love you more than we could ever say.

Acknowledgments

TO MY HUSBAND, Sekou, my mom, my sisters and brothers, my dearest friends, my editors, Jessica Wick and Stephanie Carnes, and my biggest supporters. Where would I be without you?

Thank you for all your love, all your kindness, and all your support.

The Fall of Elan

PROLOGUE

THE AMASITI HAVE always been one with the village, the earth, and life itself. From first we came, it has been our purpose to bring knowledge and wisdom to the land of Yet and all the lands beyond. We were not a part of The Way. We *were* The Way. They called us Mother, and so it was for thousands of years until the time of the Hir descended.

The talent to heal, to see, to lead was given to us by birth from the God Amalaki, handed down to each female descendant of Her bloodline, because only women have the power to create.

But for all our gifts, we did not see what was to come.

With no Mother to receive my account and no chance of living past this day, I commit the story of the fall of my city, the fall of Elan to this parchment in hopes of preserving it against the treachery and deceit of these times. So that our descendants, who must now hide within the belly of lesser shadows, will one day know and reclaim that which has been stolen.

I write to you of the future as though it is past because I know what will be. My name is Aferi, and because of what I have done, I wear the poison chains. I am the last sorcerer of Elan.

To truly understand the Amasiti, you must first understand the language of dance. To the Amasiti, the body is more than just a sacred vessel, it is a channel through which, if trained properly, wisdom and power can be found in the sway of a woman's hip. Even our greeting to each other is dance. A soft curve of the palm over the heart, fingers held just so, so that the intention is unmistakable. An open call from one Goddess to another.

The Amasiti learn to dance early with bare soles to bare earth so that there is no interruption in the flow of energy between the realm of experience, change, and creation, which is earth and the realm of wisdom and permanence in the heavens. The space between these two realms is The Way, the place where we conduct the energy of the earth and temper it with the wisdom of Amalaki to create knowledge. In dance, we become the current between the sky and the great depths below. Every fiber of our bodies, every tinkle of our bracelets is a conveyor of information gained and shared.

But we do not dance in silence. The earth and the sky sing out to us in a voice only those entrusted to keep its secrets can hear. Each of us hears a different tone, a different voice in accordance with our talents, but we all dance as one just as the leaf and the wind move with common purpose. And in that current of knowledge and wisdom comes the power to heal, the power to shape, and the power to transform.

Each movement conveys a sequence of truth that is known and understood by us alone. It is forbidden for anyone outside the Amasiti to witness our dance. We have always understood that knowledge of the dance without the ability to control the power it summons would only breed confusion and chaos, which is exactly what our world has become.

It was not always so...

There is a beauty that rests so deeply within the soul that it can only be witnessed by those who hunger for the same boundless splendor. Elan had such a soul. Elan was such a place. It was my home.

Though I am sure such people existed, I never encountered anyone who could recall a time when the glittering towers and paved roads of Elan did not shine with a brilliance that could be seen from every corner of Yet. From the last quiver of the 3rd moon to the first rise of the 2nd sun, the city could be seen clear across the wild plain of Simhar to the west and at the most distant regions of Kiveer in the south. Crowning the highest peak of a teardrop-shaped peninsula, ships used Elan's luminescence as a beacon from which to navigate. Merchants and travelers came to the city for the robust trade, then lingered to experience the wisdom imparted by the Amasiti and the way of being their wisdom inspired. As news of the city's uncommon convergence of knowledge, food, and culture spread, Elan became known as the Shore of Light, and for a long time, it was.

Because of its vitality, it is often assumed that we founded the city, but this is not true. The Amasiti did not build the city of Elan, or any other that we inhabited, though I will not deny that our influence shaped everything we touched. The Amasiti came to Elan as healers, teachers, diviners, and sages to ease the burden of mankind and keep the search for life's meaning awake in the hearts of those who would seek its truth.

We founded our first temple, The Great Temple of Amalaki, at the center of the city. Everything, from its location and round structure to the temple's vibrant tapestries, artwork, and carvings, was designed to make it easy for us to become one with the city and the city to become one with us. The Temple functioned as a home for all Mothers, a headquarters for the Amasiti, and a place of knowledge open to all who would come.

I was born in Elan's Great Temple, the third daughter of the seventh sorcerer of Elan, though truly, within the Mother's temple, I was everyone's child. My mother's love for me was made more precious by the magnitude of affection that surrounded it. I sat on every lap and proved my knowledge with anyone who would teach me. Thus was our custom, to love each child as one's own. I counted myself among hundreds of siblings throughout the sisterhood of the Amasiti and relished my childhood for as long as it lasted.

Whether through the presence of our magic or the work of our hands, we were taught to be a blessing to every community that welcomed us. In our youth, all Amasiti tilled the fields, cooked the food, washed the clothes, and fetched the water so that we understood the lives of those we served.

But, while we were loved for the fruit of our toil, we were revered for our power. At night, while those around us slept, we gained knowledge from the earth and wisdom from above through our dance, and we shaped that wisdom into a force that would serve the world.

The magic of our gifts comes differently to each of us, but one who is well-proved can often see a thread of what a child's talent will be from the time we learn to make our first words. For me, it began with the soil. Though it has been more than twenty years since I last dug a yam from the ground, I can still remember the tug of earth beneath my fingernails and the sweet smell of minerals that tickled the back of my throat. As a small child, I would sneak the dirt-caked yams into my bed at night to comfort me, driving my Mothers mad each morning.

From digging the dirt, I learned by smell which vegetables and herbs would flourish best in different fields. By seven, my talent brought me to other towns and villages to help increase their harvests and cultivate the best produce to sell at the great markets at Nehor and Seht. In gratitude, the people in towns without an Amalaki temple began to call me Aferi, which means "of the soil" in the native tongue, and it is the only name I have answered to since.

My awakening to the deeper meaning of my power came with a dream that shook the foundations of the Temple. I saw myself rising from the vast universe below, cutting through oceans, rocks and the underpinnings of our world like a shooting star. I burned hot and furious as I flew, but I welcomed the heat and the friction that spoke of my coming. I arose from the dream to find my bedsheets soaked with sweat and my clothes burned to ether. Around me the Mothers, *my* Mothers, stood before me with hands raised in prayer and welcome.

I was fourteen years old and The Mother was alive within me.

Never before had any awakening or any power of the Amasiti shook the foundations of the earth. News of my power traveled quickly on the tongues of those who witnessed and those who had merely heard the story of the Awakening of Aferi. But as the whispers of rumor and legend returned, they brought a trail of danger right to our doorstep. At least, that is what I tell myself in times when blame and guilt feel more manageable than the truth. In reality, trouble was already underfoot, like fertile soil waiting for a seed to take root and grow strong.

During their time, the Mothers brought almost as many daughters as sons into the world, but only girl children could enter into the Amasiti. So our brothers were often moved to the outer circles of the Temple or adopted as valued apprentices at the age of thirteen when we began our ordination as Amalaki priests. But even though our paths diverged, we always loved our brothers—some more than others.

When I think of my childhood, it is hard to recall a time when Safaro was not at my side. Though he was a year older, we did everything together. Pulling up weeds from the garden that I would feed him until our bellies churned. Carrying pails of water. Competing to see who could pick the most blue greens or pluck the highest sparrow fruit on the tree. In faith, he was, as all the other boys around me, a brother, but in truth, he was much more than that.

We shared our first kiss at the dawning of our adulthood and caressed our maturing bodies under the sheltering leaves of the soursop tree until we were slick and giddy with excitement. I planned to love him forever, but it was not enough.

When he asked me to marry him, I laughed. A high, breathless sound that carried no weight at all.

"What nonsense is this?" I asked, trying to squint past the sun in my eyes. I felt sure he was making fun of me, the way he always did.

It was only when I did not hear his laughter with mine that I shifted my gaze to see his face. He was not smiling back at me. I had hurt him, though with all my heart I had not meant to. Confused, I reached for him.

"Safi…what have I done? Tell me."

"Is my love a joke? I speak truly, Aferi. I want you to be with me and only me."

"I am with you. I will always be with you." I still did not understand.

"I have been accepted into the Guild of Welders. I am almost a man, Aferi."

My smile felt tentative as it tugged its way across my mouth, but I closed the distance between us. Slowly, I stroked the taut muscles of his abdomen, then rested my hand at the knot that held his pants in place. "I know," I answered, searching his face for the openness that had always been there.

His hand came over mine, hard and unmovable.

"Listen to me, Aferi. I want more than this. I want us to be together. I want someone to bear my children and raise them."

"I will have our children and we will raise them together." Slipping my hand away, I gripped his face between my palms. "You know I want this, too."

Not finding what he wanted in my eyes, he turned away.

"I want a wife, Aferi."

A bitter taste spread across my tongue, but my heart refused to focus on anything but trying to unravel the meaning behind the words I could not fathom.

"The Amasiti do not marry. You know this."

Only then did he turn to me, wild and desperate. He grabbed my hands and squeezed hard.

"Then renounce them and come with me. Be my wife!"

"Renounce them?" I felt the bile rising, mixing with the taste of fear in my mouth. "I *am* them. You ask this as if I could step out of my own skin."

His expression turned hard as he dropped my hands.

"You think because you are Amasiti that you are better than me!" he yelled.

I was not prepared to defend who I was to anyone, least of all him. Still, I tried, struggling for words I'd never had to speak before.

"I am different than you are, not better. We are meant for different things."

"Why? I could learn the dances. I know…" His voice cut off.

I did not realize that I had stepped away until Safaro extended his hand and I was out of reach.

"What do you know? Knowledge is not wisdom unless it is proved, Safi. You have not been given this power. You have other gifts."

I remember how his eyes, his whole being, seemed suddenly cast in shadows as he stared back at me.

"If you loved me as I love you, you would do this for me."

The pain swirling in my belly froze at his words, anchoring me to where I stood.

"I would never ask you to be anything other than who you are. I have loved you since I was old enough to know what love was— just as you are. I would never ask you to change. How can you ask this of me?"

"I want you to belong to me! Only me, as a wife should."

The words were like lightning in my ears, burning away something between us forever.

"I do not belong to anyone. Even in the Amasiti, we choose to be Mothers. Our first duty is always to be in possession of ourselves. It is the one thing we can never give away."

God was in me and I was my own center. Safaro walked away from me that night full of anger and hurt, and though I cried where I stood, I did not reach out and I did not waver.

He left the next morning. I did not see him again for many years, but I always knew that I would.

After Safaro left, we continued to understand our gifts and share our wisdom with those we served. Within the villages, there was no need for jealousy. All we had was shared. Because of our reputation as healers, we were rarely— if ever— feared. But for some, the events of my awakening became a herald of the Amasiti's growing power and how that power could be used in the hands of those who coveted it.

The first attack I'd ever heard of came from a village in the southern province of Kiveer. I was well into my powers by then, a woman of twenty-three years. It was said that a man, a stranger from a northern village by his garb, had touched a Mother without her permission in the market square. At first, I hardly believed it. None of us did.

The ruffian was dragged away by the crowd, but when it came time for him to be brought to the Elders for judgment, he was nowhere to be found. Rumor spread that the assailant had been an Aet, an evil spirit that vanished into thin air. But the Mothers knew that this was not so. For evil is born of the earth, the actions and consequences of man pushed out like a spitting cauldron. In our own way, we are all creators of light and darkness. A true spirit's only power is to create light and illuminate what is misunderstood. Sometimes the truth can kill, but that was not what happened in the marketplace. The trespasser only meant to take what was not his, seeking to steal the amulet worn by each Mother as a symbol of the earth's willingness to bind its power with hers. At the time, it did not occur to us that someone might have helped the criminal escape.

The Mothers pondered and prayed for clarity about what this infraction could mean. In our deliberations, our dance began to take on more rigid lines of protection and defense. More and more, we danced with our eyes open to the new possibility of prying gazes. The notion of needing to not just keep—but *defend*—our secrets was born.

But defense was not a concept that came naturally to the Amasiti. We were created to give to the world. Our training, our knowledge rituals were all done in service to the power we were given, and it was our duty to see that it was put to the best use. We served those around us with love and openness. In return, they gave us their trust, heeded our counsel, and respected our ways.

I do not know when or how word of our power—of *my* power—reached the Hir, but by the time I learned that it had, there was no uncertainty about who brought our secrets to him. There were rumors that men had stolen our dance rituals to create a new kind of power—a poison created through metal and fire—that could control or command our will.

Things began happening that had never happened before—harassment, threats, rape...murder. Mothers were rarely the victims of these attacks, but they were always the targets. By then, the Hir knew our true weakness: the people we loved and the communities we served.

And as the Hir's cruelty spread from the south, without mercy or reason, the order of the world was lost. Horror seeped into our lives until we were surrounded.

When the Hir rode into the first of the villages at the northern tip of Kiveer demanding submission of the Mothers, the Amasiti refused until we understood the price that those around us would pay for our defiance. He started with the youngest child in the village. It was as expedient as it was cruel. To protect those whom they had always served, the Mothers accepted the bondage of the poison chains that allowed the Hir and his emissaries to use the Mothers' power as their own.

Children stopped reaching for the safety of their parents' arms because they knew that their mothers and fathers could no longer protect them. Instead, we were forced to send them away, scattering our future to the wind and breaking the will of our people.

As the news of the Hir's coming spread, the villages became unsafe for the Mothers to inhabit. Those willing to break faith with the Amasiti traded their decency for the baser needs of food, shelter, and the hope of protection. Those who resisted were killed, enslaved, or tortured to madness, their lives left in ruins.

By the time the Mothers thought to use their power to fight, it was far too late. In truth, we had never organized our power into a force of destruction before. We were created by Amalaki to bring and create life. Becoming a vessel of war was unthinkable. So when the Hir began taking the Amasiti, many of the powers he sought to corrupt could not be used to his advantage, but they kept searching. Many Mothers chose to ascend from this life, which was their right as keepers of The Way, rather than see their power exploited. I could not.

I knew deep within me that the Mother had made me different for a reason. So when Safaro came for me, I was not afraid. The truth can sometimes kill and I knew that I would find a way, even if it cost me my life.

I called on each of my sisters within the Temples to send me the youngest of our awakened, all those with talents in water, earth, or anything related to animals. They were to be stripped of the blue silk gowns that would identify them as Amasiti and come to Elan alone with only a trusted male to carry them, who would pose as their father.

As I helped each of them from the carriages where they'd hidden on their long journeys, I looked into their young, guileless eyes. I had said nothing to them; yet somehow, they knew. Like me, the Mother had made them different. They arrived frightened, but determined, with just enough time to hide them before Safaro slipped past Elan's defenses disguised as the prodigal son returned.

When I finally saw him walking towards me again, I knew that almost no trace of the boy I loved had survived. His face was sunken and pock-marked from what I guessed was too much of the Hir's rich food and not enough of the grains and vegetables that keep the Amasiti strong and youthful long into our lives. He knew better but had chosen to trade what was proven for a soulless power that answered to neither knowledge nor wisdom.

I knelt before Safaro, as I swore I would never do when we were children, and accepted his chain, then watched as his pride swelled, eclipsing any possibility that he would discover my plan. Blind purpose and certain victory propelled him forward without the slightest concern for why a woman who had defied him every day of her life would have surrendered so easily. I bowed my head and followed him, prepared to betray everything I knew to preserve the hope of what we could become.

Like a slave, he brought me dutifully to his master. We snuck past the gates of Elan to the Hir who sat outside the battlefield on a tall, white horambus that was draped in blood-red velvet. The Hir spared only a second to regard me with contempt before sending me with Safaro to the center of the battle where our right to exist would be decided.

All around me, from every corner of our world, the people of Yet fought against the tyranny of the Hir. Closing my eyes, I could smell their desire to live, to protect their loved ones, and see them survive past this day as if the earth itself was calling out to me. Once again I looked to Safaro for any sign of the boy I loved, but he was nowhere to be found. He knew, as I did, that while their resolve was as hard as iron, the people of Yet were not warriors. Worse, we'd only had months to prepare. From the power-crazed look in his eyes as he surveyed the battle, I knew that the Hir had been planning the expansion of his Kingdom his entire life.

The final battle came to our doorstep just outside the city of Elan where our defenses had held as fiercely as they could, but it was only a matter of time. The people of Elan, the peoples of Yet, had given no ground easily with mounting casualties on both sides, but the Hir had too much of everything we lacked: weapons, men, strategy, and now the most powerful Amasiti at his beck and call.

With me at their side, they pressed forward. The poison chain connected my will to Safaro's, so that the power between us acted as one, except only I understood the true meaning behind the Hir's command to create an earthquake that would swallow his enemies. Safaro could wield my power, but only I could give it the purpose that would call it into being.

I knew what the Hir's soul was meant to be. His greatest enemies were not in front of him; he was surrounded by them, masking the truth of his insanity behind greed and false adulation.

And so, when I spread my hands wide and bellowed across the sky "I am the Sorcerer of Elan, now and always," I did what I was meant to do: create.

The boats of Elan were just out of range, harboring the men, women, and children who were unable to fight. Only the strongest were allowed to keep the front. It would be difficult for them to escape, but they had a better chance than anyone who was not privy to my plan.

I felt the fissure crack open far beneath me, then bubble up and break with a diagonal energy just 100 feet from where I stood. The fissure would only hold for a few minutes, announcing itself as a warning of things to come so that my people would have some time to retreat before the fault folded back on itself and consumed everything standing.

Safaro watched with satisfaction as the people of Yet began to run. He did not understand until he watched them forego the high ground of Elan and run into the sea. He rushed forward just as the fissure we created together broke open into a chasm that pulled the dirt right out from under the Hir's army.

The people of Yet scattered as the depths swallowed the Hir's front line. As soon as the last of my people were safe, I took it all. The land that held Elan to the shore of Yet fell away, allowing the water to rise up, pounding out new territory as it ripped through the battlefield. But it was not enough.

It was only then that I understood that creation and destruction are often the same thing. As the sea claimed its prize, I opened up the foundation of Elan itself—breaking it from the bottom like an egg.

The power of the sea did the rest, opening her arms to the island in an eternal embrace that left only the tip of the land visible, with the children I had left there clinging to ancient trees.

Fear, terror, and isolation had burned through their innocence, but in exchange I had given them something else—a chance to survive and create something new, to evolve into sorcerers who were also warriors.

As Safaro twisted the poison chain around my neck, I imagined I could see the eyes of all those Amasiti children and hoped only for their forgiveness.

And in the burning light of my death, I ascended to the withering screams of the Hir, Safaro, and all his murderous men and was at peace.

BY THE EVE of the 400th Anniversary of the Elan Peace Accords, the daughters of Amalaki had been hunted to the brink of extinction. Those who survived did so by hiding in plain sight while nurturing their powers in secret until the hope of Aferi could be renewed.

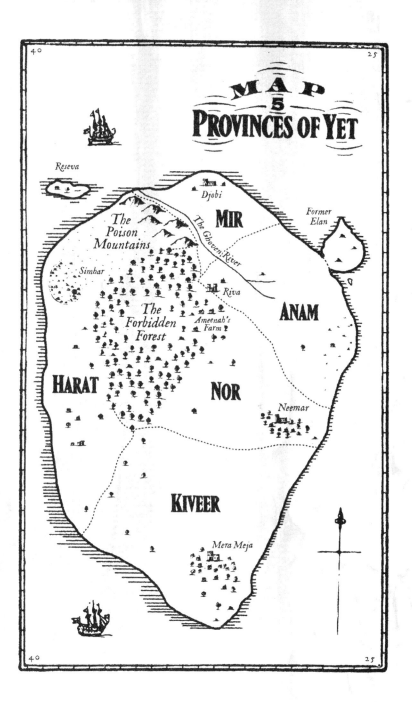

40   25

MAP
5
PROVINCES OF YET

Reseva

Djobi

The
Poison
Mountains

MIR

Former
Elan

The Ghoveni River

Simhar

ANAM

Riva

The
Forbidden
Forest

Ameenah's
Farm

HARAT

NOR

Neemar

KIVEER

Mera Meja

40   25

The Wolf Queen

BOOK I

The Hope of Aferi

CHAPTER 1

A Quiet Life

AMEENAH STEPPED OFF of her front porch and into the pale light of the first sun, finally ready to face the journey ahead. She had been looking forward to her trip to the market in Djobi for two months. Tradesmen throughout the five provinces of Yet fought over the privilege of selling her work, and she was happy to let them do so, for the right price. But the biggest market was in the city of Djobi on the northern coast of the province of Mir. Ameenah always saved the best of her wares for Djobi and carried them there herself.

The time it took to weave the coveted baskets and leather goods for which she was known was considerable, which made it impossible to manage more than two or three trips a year. But the long months in between trips were good for her. It allowed Ameenah time to gather the courage to leave her farm on the edge of the Forbidden Forest and venture out into the world.

The day of her trip, she rose before dawn and worked all morning, oiling her leathers, tightening her basket knots, and inspecting each item until she was sure it was worthy of the most discerning customer. After, Ameenah changed out of her simple brown dress into her more sturdy traveling clothes: a pair of rough cotton pants, a long-sleeved tunic, and a frayed strip of mud-cloth to hold back her hair.

Then, she loaded her wagon. The heavier baskets made of stained soursop leaves went in first, stacked on top of one another in three perfect rows that lined the frame of the wagon. Inside the top baskets, she tucked and folded her leather goods—satchels, pouches, containers, belts, pants, vests, and tunics—all as hard as wood or as supple as silk depending on what would suit their purpose best.

The cost of just one of her creations would cover a year's worth of one farmhand's wages. Anywhere else in Yet, people would have scoffed at her prices, but in Djobi, the vendors and artisans catered to wealthy traders, emissaries of royalty and high-rolling thieves who traveled to Yet's northern shores from around the world. These customers did not travel to Yet for a bargain. They came for the exceptional and offered nothing but praise for her extraordinary craftsmanship when they paid her, which was part of the reason she made the trip.

By the time Ameenah finished hoisting all her supplies and the colorful silks she would wear once she reached Djobi into the narrow aisle between her baskets, the second sun was just beginning to bath the sky in saffron light, signaling across the lush green of her home that midday was almost here. Ameenah stretched her arms to the heavens and sighed, twisting her body to coax the tension from muscles that had been lifting and bending all morning.

"The trip to Djobi will do me well." Ameenah smiled as her stomach fluttered in anticipation. The chance to earn almost half a year's income in just one day was not her only reason for making the trip. A part of her that was larger than she cared to admit hungered for the sights and sounds of the marketplace, the people she would meet, and the stories they would tell her.

Yes, I'm ready to go, she thought.

But the loud rumble in her stomach said otherwise.

When last did I eat, she wondered.

A soft chuckle in a familiar cadence rang out behind her.

With the exception of her farm manager, Opa Maru, there was no one around for miles to help her, which was exactly how Ameenah wanted it. She always left for trips on her workers' day off to avoid prying eyes. And after years of refusing his help, Opa finally stopped offering his assistance.

"You're all packed, I see," Opa said, coming to stand beside her with a sly grin. Ameenah's begrudging smile at his teasing quickly faded as the scent of injera and her favorite lentils wafted up towards her from the steaming bowl in Opa's hands.

The laugh he gave at her wide eyes, delighted her though she would never tell him so.

"I thought you might be hungry."

Ameenah rushed over to the trough of fresh water she kept just outside her front gate and cleaned her hands.

"Thank you!" she said while reaching for the bowl. Her hands were still dripping with water when she folded the first delicious bite into her mouth.

"Hmmm," Opa replied, inspecting her wagon. "You've done well. Of course, with another pair of hands to help, you could have been halfway to Djobi by now."

Ameenah lowered her eyes.

"I know," she began, hesitating over her food. "But I've told you before, I'll be traveling alone. You won't be there if I need help. I need to make sure I can manage everything on my own."

The older man answered her with eyes that were sad and silent. He knew Ameenah well enough to know she'd meant no harm, but her words still stung. They had worked together for five years with an ease between them that, on most days, felt more like family than friends. Yet, their bond had never been strong enough to break through Ameenah's instinct to hold herself at a distance from those closest to her.

"I could come with you," Opa offered gently. "The roads are not safe."

Ameenah smiled as she moved closer, allowing herself a moment to enjoy the way his arm came up to squeeze her shoulder. A part of her welcomed his company. His presence on the long road to Djobi and back would have been warm and familiar, like all the comforts she'd trained herself to do without.

Ameenah had been on her own since she was twelve years old, longer if you counted from the day her family was murdered. Life since then had not been easy, but at twenty-two, Ameenah took solace in knowing that the experience of having lost the people she loved most in the world had forced her to become a woman who could fend for herself. Though she knew Opa meant well, Ameenah couldn't afford to depend on him more than she already did.

"Thank you, Opa, truly, but I need you here to take care of things while I'm away."

Knowing there was nothing more he could do to change her mind, Opa nodded silently and said no more. When she had cleaned her bowl, Opa took it from her and bid Ameenah the Mother's blessings on her travels.

After securing the wagon, Ameenah checked the house one last time before leaving. Opa would see that the chickens were fed and the land was cared for during her three-day journey to Djobi and back, but Ameenah was nothing if not meticulous. Almost everything she cared about was in the small cottage, the fields, and the earth that she called home. Leaving it filled her with a slow, burning dread that would linger until she returned.

"Opa will watch over the place," Ameenah whispered to the deep brown and white speckled horse beside her. Shifting her eyes to the forest's edge, Ameenah sighed. "And the wolf, too." She could not explain how she knew, but Ameenah was sure that somewhere within the woods, her strange tawny friend was watching.

It began the second night after construction had finished on her farm. Everyone who had come to help was gone, leaving Ameenah in her brand-new home on her brand-new farm alone. The heavy scent of fresh-cut bamboo and acacia was sweet in the air, and Ameenah wandered the fields that night with a restless excitement. The newly-planted seedlings had barely broken through the tender soil, and Ameenah was careful of her footing as she stepped between the rows of crops with her skirt knotted high above her bare feet and ankles.

She found the wolf at the edge of where the Forbidden Forest met her field. His pale tan fur was half covered by a strange mist. His eyes were golden and clear. And though Ameenah stood transfixed by its beauty, she did not fear the animal. The wolf stood still as well, neither retreating nor moving forward until it suddenly let out a low howl, then sprinted away.

She'd seen him many times since then, always watching from the edges of her farm. Though there was no rhyme or reason to his visits, Ameenah was always glad to see him when he came.

Wolves were considered a bad omen by many in Yet; maligned as tricksters with vicious cunning and ill intent. But at the edge of the Forbidden Forest, where everything was feared, Ameenah could only see the wolf as an auspicious sign that what had been lost or cast away in other parts of the world could flourish here.

"Are you ready, Ifa?"

Ifa rustled her mane and took a step forward, testing the weight of her load before moving ahead at a pace her companion could match. Beside her, Ameenah pulled the mud-cloth from her hair, releasing the tinkling, tapping sound of metallic bells and cowry shells into the air. Then, she adjusted the belt around her waist to make sure her ivory bone dagger was within reach—just in case.

CHAPTER 2

The Way to Djobi

THE MERCHANT ROAD was by far the fastest means of travel to and from Yet's marketplaces, but expedience was rarely Ameenah's main concern, which was why she never used it. For almost every other tradesman in Yet, it was their main route for transporting goods. In addition to weaving seamlessly through most of the five provinces, the Merchant Road provided direct access to the major markets in Kiveer, Mir, Aman and Nor. The road also served as a meeting point for suppliers and other businesses that benefited from the flow of trade. The only province market without an access point on the Merchant Road was Harat, whose rulers forbade trading of any kind, except outside the gates of their southern border. Even then, tradesmen who failed to procure approval from the Harati Council to sell at their borders were killed without trial or warning.

In the early days, because everyone benefited from access to the road, security was never a cause for concern. Every merchant paid special taxes through the Craftman's Guild to maintain the road that had been in existence from too far back for anyone to recall its beginnings.

Even after the Fall of Elan, the Hir's guards traveled the road frequently, buying gifts and supplies for their families. The guards' presence helped to maintain the security of the road while acting as a subtle reminder of the Hir's influence over every aspect of life in Yet.

But with the rise of the 9th Hir, things began to change.

Strangers from other lands started to frequent the markets with no regard for their traditions and customs. Shortly after, travelers and merchants reported the first incidence of harassment and theft on the Merchant Road. In response, the Craftman's Guild increased their dues and began hiring soldiers from each of the five provinces to patrol the markets. The Guild hoped to quell the problem quickly, but with thousands of miles of road to patrol and limited resources to do so, the safety of the road continued to falter. When the costs became too great for the merchants to bear alone, the Guild reached out to the Hir for protection. Despite their pleas for help, the presence of the Hir's guards grew increasingly scarce as crime continued to fester until some within the provinces began to wonder if the Hir was using the unrest in the markets to increase his power at the expense of his people's prosperity.

The Elan Accords were supposed to give the provinces of Yet relative autonomy while still coordinating laws and resources between provinces under the overarching authority of the Hir. The 2nd Hir and the governors of all five provinces signed the treaty almost 400 years ago, shortly after the Fall of Elan. Ameenah didn't know all of the provisions, but she also didn't care. She knew how little those words meant. Many promises had been broken since those early days.

Never having lived during the relatively peaceful reign of the previous Hirs, Ameenah grew up on tales of how dangerous the road had become. Only a fool would take their safety for granted, and a woman traveling alone could never afford to be foolish. With no means or desire to curry favor with the mercenaries that sold their swords to the highest bidder, Ameenah resolved to steer clear of the road altogether. Though the trip took longer with Ameenah and Ifa weaving through the dark pathways and forest trees, it allowed them to slip past entire villages unnoticed.

If all went well, Ameenah knew the twelve-hour journey would deliver them in Djobi just before the rise of the third moon at eleven pm.

Slipping into the dense cover of the forest, Ameenah could almost hear her mother's voice.

"Meena, do you hear it?" The little girl she had been gripped her mother's hand, squeezed her eyes shut, and tried to listen harder.

Fewa knelt and pressed her lips to Ameenah's ear. Even in that moment, Ameenah could not recall hearing the sound of her mother's voice. Instead, she felt the effervescent sensation of her mother's words bubbling up through her mind.

You can never truly be lost in the forest. The trees will help you find your way.

Ameenah opened her eyes to the sound of a thousand whispers.

"Ina!" her little voice gasped. "I hear them!"

All around her, the trees felt suddenly enormous and foreboding. She could not see her mother's face, but the touch of

Fewa's warm hand was ever-present as she led them through twisted tree trunks and heavy vines that hung low enough to caress your face or crush your skull. But with her mother's guidance, she could see their terrifying beauty as well. The air around them was crisp and clean as if nothing unwanted was allowed to stay there.

Walking through the forest now, the familiar scent twisted the memory into a searing pain that Ameenah felt at the very center of her chest. Immediately, Ameenah pressed her palm against her mother's necklace just below her throat and pretended, as she always did, that she was still walking in her mother's footsteps, who was just too far ahead for Ameenah to see.

Ameenah reached the streets of Djobi just as the third moon approached its summit. Despite the loss of daylight, the crowd was lively, with merchants determined to sell their wares by moonlight if it meant taking a greater share of money from customers who drank more and haggled less. Ameenah saw many she knew, but none she wanted to talk with just then. There would be time enough for pleasantries in the morning. Still keeping out of sight, Ameenah took Ifa to the only stable she trusted her with, then slipped into the back door of her favorite inn to rest and prepare herself for the day ahead.

Whether you liked it or not, Djobi by daylight was always something to see. Established along the rugged cliffs of Yet's northeastern coast, the city was built in a hurried attempt to replace the trading port lost during the Fall of Elan. Djobi was known as much for its crowded, uneven streets as for its brightly colored banners and sails that bellowed from every window and building top, beckoning sailors from afar to rest at its shores.

Though most structures displayed the ash wood or green-grey indigenous stone from which they were made, it was not uncommon for some business owners to paint the facades of their storefronts in bright oranges, reds, and yellows to complement their banners. The festive colors and music blaring from the balconies and rooftops of Djobi's two-story buildings had the effect of making the casual visitor feel perpetually open to seduction.

While some deemed Djobi a lesser cousin to the legend of Elan, Ameenah recalled that her mother had always taken deep offense to the comparison. With no frame of reference, Ameenah had only thought of Djobi as a good place to do business until two years earlier when she took a rare walk past the marketplace to explore the city. Five streets over from the marketplace, she walked onto the street they called the "Fishnet." Immediately, Ameenah understood why.

Women and men in varying stages of undress poured from every doorway and window with their arms stretched out to catch whoever came within arm's reach. In one house, the fullest from what Ameenah could see from the open windows of the tavern, a large woman sat at the front door. She was naked save for a white flower that hung low behind her ear. Her plump hands rested gently on her knees, which were spread open with one leg propped high on a stool. Shocked, Ameenah met the woman's eyes and found herself immediately pulled in by the most comely smile she had ever seen. When Ameenah was unable to speak, the woman's left eyebrow slowly rose to a crest. Ameenah could not resist answering her challenge with a bashful smile before hurrying away. It was only then that Ameenah understood Djobi's true appeal as a place where desire in all its forms was allowed to run through the streets with abandon.

Ameenah rose in darkness. Set-up under the purple banners that were reserved for the most high-end goods usually began at sunrise, but Ameenah completed many of her sales well before then. By the time Ameenah delivered the custom orders from her previous trip and arrived at her stall, a quarter of her inventory was gone. Then came the Craftman's Guild's tradition of trading and purchasing amongst each other before the selling day began. Ameenah made custom items for this group as well, which she traded for the best medicines from the Kingdom of Ema and spices from as far east as Jor.

After all, the men and woman of the Guild had been good to her. First, they offered her a coveted seat on their Council due to the exceptional quality and popularity of her work among Djobi's most wealthy patrons. Then, they allowed her to continue selling with them under the honored purple banners when she refused to take the position. Though she kept a safe distance from the politics and prying she knew would inevitably accompany closer association, Ameenah held most of them in favorable regard.

In fact, Ameenah had a good relationship with almost every vendor in the marketplace except Beln Amin, who happened to hold the stall right next to hers.

"Blessings to you, Sha Min Beln," Ameenah announced as a stable boy borrowed from the inn secured Ifa and her wagon to her stall post. Since Beln was bent down and fussing over her only son, Yosi, Ameenah was not sure the woman heard her. Ameenah used Beln's brief distraction to nod a greeting to the rest of the Amin family. Yosi looked back at Ameenah with playful eyes, smiling at the woman his mother called "a bad influence." Yosi wasn't sure exactly what that meant, but this bit of information only made Yosi like Ameenah more. Beside him, Sa Min Sisay returned Ameenah's nod while chuckling at his son's open fascination.

In service to his silent admiration, Yosi's hand rose up in a discreet little wave while his mother tugged at the hem of his pants. Ameenah smiled but didn't dare wave back.

"You're growing too fast! Go play," Beln said with a kiss on Yosi's round cheeks and a smile that Ameenah could hear through the deep affection in her voice. "But stay close to your father."

Beln watched her family walk out into the sun and down the promenade with a wistful hand over her heart. Ameenah smiled after them too, knowing how well Beln loved them. But by the time she returned her attention to her neighbor, the woman was staring back at her as if she were a soiled rag.

"Hhummh," Beln huffed.

"You look well," Ameenah offered as she turned to retrieve her supplies. Despite Beln's mean disposition towards everyone but her family, Ameenah thought the woman had a pleasant face, round and smooth despite her years, when it wasn't pinched up in a scowl. "I wish you good fortune today."

Beln made the finest coffee blends in all of Yet, and though Ameenah had wished her blessings for the day, she knew the woman would not need it.

There. I've tried, Ameenah thought, as she unfolded her embroidered yellow silk tablecloth and shook it out over her front table. When the Guild representative warned her that she would be side-by-side with Beln in the craftman's stalls, it had taken Ameenah more than a moment to figure out how she was going to deal with her. The necessity of talking to potential customers all day was daunting enough. Ameenah would need all her good graces for the day ahead. She couldn't spare any more effort trying to get along with the ornery woman.

"Still no husband, I see."

Ameenah ignored her. From her past experience, she knew that Beln was far from finished. But the older woman did not continue her insults right away, extending the blessed silence between them as she became engrossed in some new task Ameenah refused to acknowledge. Ameenah had almost managed to forget their entire conversation before the woman spoke again.

"A girl must have some family who can speak for her," the woman muttered with her back to Ameenah. "How a mother leaves her own daughter without a match, to wander the world like a stray dog, I will never understand."

"Sha Min! My mother died when I was little. I've explained this to you already," Ameenah replied. Though the woman's back was to her, she tried her best to keep the irritation from her voice and expression.

Beln turned around with a plate of food in her hands and a cup of steaming, fresh coffee. Her light brown eyes were skeptical.

"Eat this. The Mother only knows how you survive on your own."

This was the reason why no matter how insensitive Beln was to her, Ameenah could never allow herself to get too angry. In her own twisted way, even Beln cared for her.

"Thank you, Sha Min," Ameenah replied, eyes downcast. "You needn't worry for me. I manage well enough on my own." Just then, her stomach growled loudly.

Of course, Ameenah sighed.

"Hummph," was Beln's only response as she turned around and all but ignored Ameenah for the rest of the morning.

As the first sun rose higher in the sky, Ameenah worked quickly to finish arranging her table for the customers who were already beginning to wander through. She draped leather tunics and belts in between intricately-woven baskets and flashes of bright silk that were designed to entice the eye and loosen the purse strings.

But while she decorated her table with seemingly effortless flair, inside Ameenah could feel her nerves wrestling with Beln's breakfast in her stomach. Usually, she didn't like to eat before mid-day when she was in Djobi, but to keep whatever fragile peace there could be with Beln, she took the food and ate it gratefully.

I only have to sell for today, she assured herself. With any luck her sales would go quickly, ensuring a swift and weightless journey home.

May the Mother's blessing shine upon me this day, she prayed, then turned toward the growing crowd with a smile.

CHAPTER 3

The Dancing Fish

MORNING SALES CREPT along slowly as the cool breeze and hot sun tempted buyers to linger and chat longer than usual, but Ameenah was content. She'd already talked to more people in the last hour then she'd seen in the past five months. It was never easy for her, but over the years, she had perfected the art of smiling and waiting, answering a question or two then letting her work speak for itself as she listened to her customers share tales from lands so far away, she doubted she'd ever have the chance to visit them.

Some stories were epic, the unveiling of a grand adventure that somehow ended at her table. Others were as personal as the way the surface of a garment reminded a customer of their lover's caress. Every time she sold an item made from her own hand, Ameenah couldn't help but feel she'd somehow become a part of the adventure of their lives.

Despite the leisurely pace of the day, Ameenah was surprised to find more than half her goods had been sold by the time the second sun reached its summit. Most of the customers had been pleasant, too, with the exception of two gruff men who bought several belts to replace the ones that could no longer contain their girth. They talked only amongst themselves, remarking on the quality of her work with lewd references, as if she wasn't there, then threw down their money without so much as a hello or a goodbye. Watching them stride away with their air of supreme importance, Ameenah doubted their twisted mouths even remembered the shape of the words, "thank you."

Soon enough, her thoughts of the rude men were washed away by a kind tradesman from the western isle of Reseva who came by, as he always did, to buy new clothes for his sons. Ameenah's whole body shook with laughter as the man regaled her with the latest tales of his children's misdeeds while imagining how one of her leather vests would be received by the son for whom it was intended. She was in the middle of wrapping his purchases and bidding him farewell when she caught a shattering glint of brilliant light out of the corner of her eye and the hint of dark clove cigarettes in the air.

Oorala Safinoh of the Hibu Lands wore a tear–shaped diamond pendant as large as a walnut and as clear as polished glass on a strip of thin black leather around her neck. Few would dare to wear a stone so precious on a mere strand of leather. Fewer still would parade it around, but Oorala was wholly unconcerned. With her Tachi sword at her side and the gem attached to the finely braided necklace she'd commissioned from Ameenah herself, Oorala knew the jewel around her neck was as safe as could be.

"Three wars, four continents, and at least a dozen barroom brawls," Oorala announced as the merchant at Ameenah's table thanked her again for the small discount she'd given him and hurried on to his next appointment.

With a small smile, Ameenah faced the only woman she truly considered a friend.

"Not a scratch on them," Oorala continued as she spread her arms and turned around to display the well-worn beauty of her laced-up leather pants.

"And then, on the last stop through the Narrows a clumsy inn-keeper and a bucket of tar did them in." Oorala shifted to the side for emphasis. Ameenah could barely make out two very small dribbles of black tar on the side lacing that ran up the woman's pants. As tiny as the spots were, to Oorala, they were enough.

"Did the innkeeper survive?" Ameenah asked with an arch of her brow. The infamous captain of the *Red Dawn* was not known for her mercy.

Oorala perched her slim frame on the edge of Ameenah's front table and sighed.

"Just a cut across the chest was all I had time for, I'm afraid." Oorala's smile was wicked as she traced a delicate "X" mark across her small torso while balancing her cigarette in her hand. "He was lucky to crawl away with his life. If he'd been on the *Red Dawn*, I'd have fed him to Benbe. You look good, by the way, but I can tell you're still not getting laid."

After a long drag, Oorala put her cigarette out with the heel of her boot.

Ameenah closed her eyes against the flush that rose up her cheeks. "Obnoxious as ever," she replied, but her smile betrayed her affection. "It's good to see you, too, Oorala."

The corner of Oorala's eyes crinkled with mirth as she let out a deep-throated laugh. "Nothing I say ever shocks you. I have missed you as well."

The women hugged each other for a long time in silence before Oorala stepped away and took a look at Ameenah's table.

"I should have come earlier. You've been busy," Oorala mumbled as she walked around admiring the bags and tunics that remained. "So lovely," she murmured as she picked up a leather vest that was at least two sizes bigger than she could wear. "Do you have anything left for me in your den of treasures?"

Before Oorala could finish, Ameenah brought out a large package that she'd tucked away at the back of her stall.

"I must have known you'd need a new pair of pants," she said softly as she put the package down on the table and stepped away. Oorala's eyes grew as big as a child's before she grabbed the package and loosened the ribbon that held the delicate leather fabric together. Oorala was silent as her hand traced her new clothes, a pair of fine leather oilskin pants in burnished black and brown and a matching tunic unlike any she'd ever seen. The tunic's arms were wide and loose with intricate cut-outs along the hems and fringes, as detailed and fine as lace with a torso that tapered at the waist into a delicate flute shape.

"They're just beautiful," she sighed before shifting her attention back to her friend. "Thank you."

Ameenah turned away, beaming with so much pride and affection that she felt embarrassed. "How is Benbe?" she asked in an attempt to regain her composure.

"He misses you," Oorala replied. As if sharing the same thought, they both glanced over her shoulder towards the large "No Animals" sign that hung at the front of the marketplace entrance. The roughly drawn sign featured an "X" over the image of a large lizard.

They knew it well because Oorala was the reason the Guild had put it there.

Oorala used to bring Benbe with her wherever she went until a merchant tried to cheat Oorala out of the proper weight of spice for which she had paid. Sensing her displeasure, Benbe— all twelve feet of him—nearly swallowed the disreputable man whole. After throwing the merchant out on his rear, the Craftman's Guild threatened to sell Benbe's skin and ban Oorala from the market forever if she ever brought him out again, but she still got twice the weight she paid for in spices as an apology for the offending merchant's behavior.

Despite all her many adventures, Oorala confided to Ameenah later that it had been one of the few times in her adult years that she'd ever been frightened. Most people would easily mistake Benbe for a lizard—a very large and terrifying example of its species, but a lizard nonetheless. Under this premise, one might assume that if you avoided the teeth inside his elongated mouth, you should be safe. Unfortunately, Benbe was not a lizard.

Years ago, she told Ameenah the story of how they first met.

Oorala had been born in a city called Mobet, cast aside as an orphan of barely five years old when her parents were murdered for being unable to pay the rent for the single room they shared. The landlord sold her to the mines as a way to recoup his losses. Alone, with no one to care for her, Oorala survived on the bugs and leaves that she could find in the low hills outside the mines and fell asleep to the sound of her own prayers mixed in with the clash of men fighting each other to death over the scraps of food their employers provided. For a year, Oorala prayed to her ancestors, hoping that someone would save her until finally she stopped believing that anyone could.

But at the age of six, Oorala learned that angels truly did exist.

Oorala discovered Benbe in the crevice of a sapphire mine. With a protruding belly and wide green eyes that shone like glass, Oorala thought he was cute. He was barely a foot long and the soft fur that covered his hard underbelly made him perfect for wrapping around her neck to keep warm while working in the cold depths.

When Oorala discovered that Benbe loved the same leaves and bugs that she did, their bond was sealed. After work, she hid him inside her tattered jacket and showed him all her favorite, secret-safe places to sleep. Benbe had become her friend and in her heart, Oorala hoped that she could be his family.

But despite her strong will to live, even for someone so young, Oorala couldn't work fast enough to avoid the cruelty of the foremen who managed the mines. Each day, she dug precious gems from the dirt. Within the darkness of the caves, Oorala could still discern the putrid silhouettes of those the foremen had beaten to death for failing to produce their daily weight in stones. Their remains were a constant source of anxious motivation that kept Oorala digging until her fingers bled. Then, if her daily quota was not met, she'd simply covered them with her shirt-sleeves and work some more.

It was not enough.

On her last day in the mines, Oorala collapsed from working all day with no breakfast and no dinner the night before. Both she and Benbe were famished.

Baloc, the head foreman, who had won his new position by killing his predecessor the night before, yanked Oorala up by the back of her neck as he cursed her for her laziness.

"I'm not gonna feed anyone who's not working," he growled.

If the attack had happened a year ago, when she first arrived at the mine, she would have cried, but Oorala knew that she was going to die. She'd seen others beg for their lives before and it had done them no good. Her tiny body dangled from the cruel man's hands as she stared into her only friend's large green eyes.

Oorala did not see him spring forward. In fact, she could not recall even the perception of movement. But suddenly she was on the ground while her captor screamed out in pain as a whirlwind of green and black scales emerged. Using the previously-hidden barbs of his long tail, the lizard that was no lizard wound his way up the foreman's body, slicing chunks of flesh away from the bone as he climbed. Flexing the down of his long belly, Benbe revealed the serrating ridges beneath, then used the sharp bone on the ridge of his nose to cut a hole under the foreman's ribs and burrow inside. The beast continued up the man's body, occasionally peeking out to flick chunks of flesh and organs to the ground.

Baloc barely had a chance to react before his head fell to the ground beside Oorala with her strange lizard friend circling the open crevice of his skull like a dancing crown of scales. Benbe emerged covered in blood and bile with a curious tilt of his head and a brand-new appreciation for the taste of flesh.

"Benbe," she whispered, recalling the word used for "angel" in her mother's tongue. Oorala rose to her knees with a smile as the creature waddled towards her with legs that strained against the weight of his stomach. Benbe retracted the claws from his tail as Oorala gently picked him up and settled him back around her neck where he burped and fell fast asleep. She walked out of the mine that day a free girl who was never afraid of anything or anyone again. It was much later that Oorala discovered that Benbe was not a lizard at all, but an irak from the Isle of Blood.

"I've missed him, too," Ameenah said softly. "He has the gentlest eyes."

Oorala laughed as she recalled how Ameenah had not shown the slightest fear as Benbe stomped up to her stall and nuzzled her knee with the blunt edge of his snout when they first met.

"Only you would say that. It takes months for you to get up the courage to be around your own kind, but deadly animals suit you just fine!"

Ameenah thought about the wolf that she had befriended outside her farm and smiled, offering no words in her defense.

"Ah, I have something for you." Oorala reached into the small black satchel that she had bought during their first meeting and pulled out a small rectangular bottle of thick purple dye. Carefully, she handed the bottle to Ameenah who cradled it in both palms.

"Where did you get this?"

"On the other side of the world," Oorala replied as she stepped closer. Ameenah held the glass bottle up to the sun and watched in awe as the liquid cast purple light across their arms and faces. She could only imagine the story that went with Oorala's gift.

The Pearl Rose was one of the rarest flowers in the world. Although there had been reports of it being found on almost every continent, no one had ever collected more than a handful in the last 200 years. The tiny lotus-shaped flower was named for its leaves that shimmered in creamy iridescent shades, from seashell white to the barest of pink blushes. When the leaves were crushed, the inner flesh bled a deep, pure purple. The dye made from the Pearl Rose leaves was worth a fortune in gold and furs because a tiny batch of dye took more than five years to make. The process involved picking thousands and thousands of tiny pearl rose petals and distilling their essence into the perfect consistency. The existence of the dye itself would have become legend if not for the unmistakable color it left on ancient artifacts and holy temples. But now, Ameenah had an entire bottle in her hand.

"I couldn't…" Ameenah began.

"You will," Oorala replied.

"This…it's too much."

"Don't be silly. I have no use for such a thing!" Oorala waved her hand dismissively as she shimmied her way out of Ameenah's booth.

Ameenah and Oorala had stopped exchanging money years ago. Instead, they chose to present each other with gifts that represented an affection and friendship neither woman was accustomed to.

"I'll see you at dinner tonight. You know where. And let's make it early. You'll be sold out soon." Oorala turned around with her eyebrow cocked and her rosebud lips pursed in defiance.

Realizing that this had been Oorala's purpose all along, Ameenah could only shake her head.

"You'll be all right," Oorala said more seriously. "I'll be right beside you the whole time. I promise."

From the front door of The Dancing Fish, Ameenah studied the faces of everyone inside. There were fellow merchants and customers who wore her clothing, but these facts did nothing to comfort her. The entire tavern was bursting with mayhem, and at the center of it all was Oorala. Standing on top of a table with a cup of honey wine in her hand and Ameenah's new outfit hugging her every curve, all eyes were on her. And, from what Ameenah could see, Oorala didn't mind at all.

Oorala was beautiful by any standard, with thick, deep brown hair that hung in perfumed waves down her back, a heart-shaped face dusted with freckles across her nose and cheeks, and arched eyebrows that framed her bright hooded eyes perfectly. Though she was short and small, her breasts and hips asserted themselves into a silhouette that was deceptively soft and supple. Nothing but the curved Tachi sword at her hip and the irak at her side gave anything of the lethal creature she truly was away.

Ameenah used the crowd's attention to her advantage, disappearing into the shadows at the corners of the room until Oorala's keen eyes spotted her.

"Another round of wine!" Oorala announced to raucous applause before descending from the table and making her way to the far end of the tavern. There she found Ameenah, hiding and only slightly terrified.

"Just for a little while," she whispered, grabbing Ameenah's hand and giving it a tight squeeze.

Ameenah took a deep breath and stepped forward, knowing that Oorala understood what it meant for her to be there.

Casually, Oorala sauntered through the crowded room, catching the men's eyes as they appraised the two woman openly. Behind her, Ameenah kept her eyes focused on Benbe's wagging tail and the two seats he was clearly guarding for them.

"See, I brought you a date," Oorala joked as Ameenah reached down to stroke the beast.

"How did you get him in here?" Ameenah asked over the crowd.

"I rented the whole place for the night." Oorala laughed wickedly. "For the right price, you can get anyone to ignore anything."

Once seated, Oorala introduced Ameenah to the guests at her table, which included the latest crewmembers on her ship, the *Red*

Dawn, and other tradesmen with whom she had business. It took a while, but eventually Ameenah settled down enough to nibble her meal and enjoy the stories they shared of their adventures and near escapes on the open seas. Though some tried to hide their profession, Oorala was a proud pirate. Living however she chose, wherever she wanted to go.

Relaxed from the warmth of the room and the sweet bite of the honey wine, Oorala leaned over to her friend.

"I'm on the hunt for a new morsel to taste before I leave in the morning, but I don't see anyone worth having."

Ameenah was about to concur when the sound of a clearing throat from behind drew their attention.

"Ameenah?"

Both women turned at the sound of the sultry voice.

"I would never have thought to find you in such a place."

"Rahmeel? What are you doing here?" Ameenah asked, rising to give him the customary greeting of one kiss on each cheek. "It's been so long."

"It has," he agreed. "I can't remember the last time we laid eyes on each other."

Unsure of how to continue the conversation, Ameenah asked the only thing she truly wanted to know. "Is Nasir with you?"

The subtle hope in Ameenah's voice took Oorala by surprise as Rahmeel's smooth brown features broadened with delight.

"Nasir? My little brother would never come with me to a place like this. I am alone. Here on business," he added as he caught a pair of lustful eyes raking over him with obvious appreciation. "But the fact that you asked for him will make his entire year. Nasir is under the sad impression that you do not care for him."

While Ameenah looked away in embarrassment, Rahmeel redirected his attention towards Oorala.

"Good evening," he purred. "My name is Rahmeel Ebibi of Nor. I'm an old friend of Ameenah's."

Oorala watched as Rahmeel took hold of her free hand, then guided it to his lips.

"Captain Oorala Sanifoh of the *Red Dawn*," she replied, savoring the softness of his skin on hers. "And here I thought Ameenah didn't have any friends."

"How fortunate for us both that this is not the case," Rahmeel replied.

The lingering touch of their hands told Ameenah that Oorala's search for the evening had concluded.

Oorala laughed with delight. "How did you get in here? This is supposed to be a private party."

"Being a representative on the Hir's Council allows me certain access, I'm afraid." Then Rahmeel leaned in as if to share a secret. "It wasn't easy, but I can be *very* persuasive."

"I'd have to be convinced of that," Oorala smirked.

"It would be my honor," he replied.

Ameenah rolled her eyes in chagrin. *He hasn't changed from when we were small. If seducing women was a profession, Rahmeel would be the richest man in the world! At least he's met his match. When Oorala's done with him, she'll leave him right where he stands,* she thought with a smirk. Seeing the opportunity to make her exit, Ameenah took a step back, into a hard unyielding surface.

She turned to find a man draped in fine grey and black linen. Though his clothing was the same style as Rahmeel's rich tan garb, the man wore a strange brooch of fire, metal and stone that was distinct enough to strike a memory she could not place from long ago. Ameenah's fingers crept close to her dagger.

"Pardon the interruption. Are you the girl they call Ameenah?"

Though his words were cordial, his voice was like ice, biting and wholly unpleasant. The flirtatious mood that had settled around their table evaporated like dew.

Before Ameenah could answer, Oorala stepped to her side.

"What is it to you?" Oorala asked. Her hand tightened on the hilt of her sword. Benbe growled low as his massive head shoved Rahmeel aside. Ameenah could hear the talons on his tail scraping the floor behind them.

"I am an officer of the Hir," the man replied, looking down with alarm at the irak that gazed back at him. "I am looking for the maker of this belt."

"Why?" Oorala demanded. The man frowned at her obvious disregard for his position.

"It is very unusual. The finest leather work I've seen. I... meant to inquire if the maker had anymore for sale."

Ameenah could not understand why, but her instincts told her that the man's interest in the belt was more than he told. His fingers seemed to molest the garment in his hand, rubbing and squeezing it obsessively.

"Jogg, please," Rahmeel interrupted. Gingerly, he moved between the unsettling man, Benbe, and Ameenah. "This is a party. Obviously no one is selling anything at this hour."

Undeterred, Jogg pushed forward. "I could visit you at your stall tomorrow."

"I don't have any more. I sold the last one this afternoon," Ameenah finally said, working hard to resist the overwhelming urge to rescue her belt from his grip.

"And you make these yourself?" he asked. The intensity of his gaze on her as he waited for her response seemed out of place given the simplicity of the question, but Ameenah could not stop herself from taking offense.

"Of course! Every member of the Craftman's Guild does," she replied.

"I see. Perhaps you have a shop I could visit to commission a piece?"

"Ameenah only sells her work in Djobi," Oorala offered. "You'll have to come back later or see if you can strike a bargain with whomever you got that belt from. You're clearly attached," she added with a repulsed shiver.

Oorala tracked Jogg's eyes as they shifted from Ameenah, to her, then Rahmeel and finally to the table of men and woman behind her who stood ready to kill him at the slightest nod of her head.

If he's smart, Oorala thought, *he'll realize that Benbe will get to him well before the rest of us.*

Oorala could almost see the moment when Jogg's mind settled into the same conclusion. His eyes settled warily on Benbe, who was salivating in anticipation of the meal before him.

"Yes, I see. My apologies for disturbing you." Jogg nodded toward Ameenah stiffly then turned to Rahmeel. "I will see you at the next Council meeting." The men exchanged a tense stare before Jogg turned and slipped back into the crowd with the belt firmly in his grasp.

"Is that cretin with you?" Oorala asked as she tracked Jogg's movements out the door. She felt a brief squeeze of her hand as Rahmeel fumbled for an explanation.

"One can't always choose who one works with," he answered sheepishly.

Unimpressed, Oorala sought out the one voice she wanted to hear.

"Ameenah, are you all right?" But by the time she turned to check, her hand was empty and her friend was gone. Briefly, Oorala thought of going to find her, but she knew she would never succeed. Beyond the shores of Djobi, her knowledge of Yet was limited. Ameenah had been hiding all her life and she was good at it.

Oorala frowned, then turned back to Rahmeel.

"Will he be able to find her?" she asked.

"I don't even know where she lives, and I think that's exactly the way Ameenah wants it."

CHAPTER 4

Unspoken Truth

AMEENAH WAITED IN the shadows, watching the man Rahmeel called Jogg turn left from the Fishnet as he headed away from the marketplace. And as she feared, he still held the belt she'd made firmly in his hand. Distracted by the perverse way he'd caressed it, it took Ameenah a moment to recall the portly man she'd sold it to earlier. Compared to Jogg's unsettling presence, she almost remembered the rude man fondly.

"I hope he got a good price for it," she thought. The belt had been one of her favorites.

Ameenah followed Jogg all the way to the steps of the Al Mar, one of the most expensive inns in Djobi, then waited an extra thirty minutes to make sure no one was following her before heading back to the stables where Ifa waited to begin their journey home.

Normally, she traveled from Djobi atop her horse, but Ameenah felt too shaken for the speed of such a trip. What she needed now was cool earth beneath her feet and time to let the image of Jogg's hand around her belt and the haunting expression he wore when he asked her if she'd made it drain from her mind like dirty water from a basin.

What did he really want?

Ameenah couldn't say when she would return to Djobi, but she knew instinctively that it would be a long time. Her only regret was not saying a proper goodbye to Oorala and Benbe, but, deep down, Ameenah knew her friend would understand.

For a moment, Ameenah wondered if she could trust Rahmeel, then eventually decided he would protect her as well as he could. Although he was nothing like Nasir, she felt fairly certain he could be counted on to keep what little he knew about her secret.

Ameenah planned to make only one stop on her way home. After her mother's death, Siama had taken her in and raised her until Ameenah insisted on making a life of her own. But Ameenah still checked in on her regularly and regarded Siama as a beloved member of the only family she had left. Siama would be expecting later, but with any luck, Ameenah would make it to Siama's house just after the second moon rose, visit for a bit, then walk through the night until she was home.

It took four hours of walking to the gentle sound of her mother's beads swinging in her hair for Ameenah to finally reclaim her sense of peace. Though the darkness might have worried other travelers, she had always enjoyed exceptional eyesight. Whether during the day or night, she could see for miles around her. Sometimes she preferred the darkness. At home, whenever she couldn't sleep, Ameenah wandered for hours listening to the strange music of night creatures.

Stepped into the clearing at the edge of Siama's home, her heart warmed at the sight of candlelight flickering through the curtains of the small cabin. The aroma of something spicy and warm beckoned as Ameenah secured Ifa to a nearby tree. She knocked gently on the door and waited.

"It's already open. Come in, child!"

Ameenah smiled as she went inside, carrying three packages under her arm.

"I thought you would be sleeping," Ameenah chided, setting the packages down on the well-worn center table. "Why are you still up?"

"My sleep is off of late," Siama replied, slowly stirring a pot on the fire. "Besides, I heard you coming."

Though Siama had yet to turn around, Ameenah was happy to use the time to take her in. The woman before her looked healthy, back straight with strong legs and bearing despite her seventy-eight years of life. Ameenah was also pleased to see that Siama did not look like she had lost any weight since her last visit six months ago. When Siama finally turned and smiled, her short white hair shown like a halo around her head, surrounding a bright face with skin as taut and shiny as a new copper pot.

"You sound like your mother," Siama said before walking towards Ameenah and giving her a warm hug. As much as the comparison startled her, Ameenah had no reason to doubt her. Siama was one of the only people left in the world who had known her mother well enough to make such a claim.

Ameenah kept her voice steady as she released herself from their embrace. "How do you mean?"

Slowly, Siama reached up and touched Ameenah's hair, fingering the bells and cowry shells within them. Ameenah had added
some from her mother's collection, others had been with her for
longer than she could remember. As if reading her thoughts, Siama
answered.

"Your mother put the first ones in before you could stand on your
own. These are no mere decorations, child. The sound they make
warns bad spirits to keep away while drawing good things near.
They are for your protection."

Siama had never told her this before and for a moment Ameenah
didn't know what to think, what to believe. All she had ever wanted
to do was be like her mother and walk in her footsteps, but the
look on Ameenah's face was clearly skeptical.

Siama sucked her teeth at the disbelief in Ameenah's eyes and
wondered, as she often did when remembering the promise she
made so long ago, whether she had made the right decision. *There
is so much you don't know about the old ways, and now it's too dangerous to tell you,* Siama thought

"No one believes in such things anymore, Siama. Besides, there
is no danger. Ifa and I made it here just fine."

The older woman pursed her lips. "No trouble?"

"No trouble."

"And how was Djobi? Did you make enough to keep you from
that horrid place for another six months at least?"

"Better," Ameenah replied, happy to change the subject. "Come.
I bought you some new clothes, medicines, salts from Kush, Beln's
ground coffee, and that ointment you like for your foot. This time
you won't run out."

Siama thanked her as she looked over the gifts Ameenah had
brought her before putting them away carefully in the baskets
beneath her bed.

"Come and eat," Siama said when she was done.

While they sat together, Ameenah ate her fresh bowl of red lentil soup alone. Having eaten her dinner hours earlier, Siama made the soup especially for Ameenah, and nothing in her day gave her greater joy than sitting down to watch her enjoy it.

Though Siama tried to let Ameenah eat in peace, her curiosity finally got the better of her.

"You're here early," Siama began. "You must have sold everything you brought with you."

Unable to break away from even a mouthful of Siama's delicious food, Ameenah grunted in agreement.

Siama beamed with pride. "Again! My! Your work has become quite popular." At seeing Ameenah's blush, Siama reached out and grabbed her arm. "Do not be bashful. You deserve this! You're nearly as talented as your mother."

"I wish," Ameenah mumbled, her mouth full of food. She still had two of her mother's handmade shawls and could attest to the fact that Siama's praise was not fully deserved. Ameenah was proud of what she could do, but her mother's work was still the finest fabric she'd ever seen, with threads woven so closely together that they looked like one solid piece of material.

"Good enough to fetch nearly a year's wages in one trip! I don't know if even your mother could have done that! What you lack is only because she is not here to teach you. You're still—"

"Oh! I almost forgot to tell you!" Ameenah blurted out, cutting Siama off before the conversation became too painful to bear. "I ran into Rahmeel at The Dancing Fish. He was there with one of the Hir's men who wanted me to sell him a belt."

Siama let the previous conversation slip away as her eyes narrowed in suspicion.

"And did you? Sell him one?"

"No," Ameenah continued. "I didn't have any more to sell. One of my customers must have shown him the belt and he liked it so much, he brought it to show me that he wanted one of his own. He seemed desperate to get his hands on one, but like I said, I didn't have any more. He was odd, anyway."

"And what did he do with the belt after you told him no?"

"He kept it. Bought it from the customer who lent it to him, I guess. Why?

"What did this man look like?"

For some reason, Ameenah felt more comfortable with this line of questioning. It made her feel more angry than afraid.

"He was tall. Gaunt. Almost ghoulish, really. He wore the same style of dress as Rahmeel and other noblemen I've seen, but in a fine greyish-black weave. He had this strange pin on his lapel, too. It looked like fire burning stone. Is that one of the Hir's symbols? I try not to keep up with anything to do with him. I have no idea how Rahmeel can even stand to be so close to the Hir and all his despicable men. I know they think that they can maintain the peace, but I just don't see how."

As Ameenah rambled on, Siama grew silent, retreating into a painful past that seemed to be rushing forward.

"It's not a new symbol. It is very old," she murmured.

"What did you say? I'm sorry, Siama. I've just been rambling on and on."

What can I tell her that will save her now? I promised never to say anything.

"The Hir's men are dangerous. You're right not to trust them. There have been reports of raids in the north and the west. Lawless men who take what they want and leave nothing behind. You need to be careful, Ameenah. Stay here tonight. You can leave at first light."

"Those are mostly just rumors," Ameenah mumbled, trying to reassure herself. "What could the Hir want with us? He already has power over everything."

Siama sighed. "For men like the Hir, there is no such thing as too much power. You must listen to me."

Ameenah had never been afraid to travel alone, but the look on Siama's face made her want to ease the woman's fears.

"I'm sorry," she said. "I shouldn't have said anything. I've worried you needlessly. If it will make you feel better, I'll stay."

Relieved, Siama took a moment to sit back in her chair and regard the girl before her—tall and strong like her mother, but with muscles her mother had never had to develop. And unlike the child she had been, Ameenah had grown from a girl who could barely wash her own clothes to a woman who could manage life on her own. A woman who—despite the demons nipping at the edges of her memory—could keep herself safe from the world outside her door.

She is nothing like the frightened little girl I first took in, Siama mused before rising from her table to prepare a place by the fire for Ameenah to sleep.

"So, you saw Rahmeel," Siama said. "I wish Nasir had been there as well."

Ameenah swallowed the lump in her throat at the mention of his name and concentrated on carrying her dishes to the washing pail by the fire.

"How do you know he wasn't?" Ameenah replied, scrubbing feverishly.

Siama cackled at her pitiful attempt at indifference.

"If Nasir had met you at The Dancing Fish, he would be sitting right there." Siama pointed to the empty seat she left behind before continuing. "Eating my food right next to you. He would never have let you travel this far alone."

Ameenah shifted awkwardly around the hearth, stacking the damp plates and bowls in a neat pile.

"I wouldn't have allowed him to come," she replied.

"And *he* would not have paid *you* any mind."

Hours before dawn, Ameenah left Siama's house on Ifa's back, feeling rested and ready to return to the seclusion of her home. But when she arrived, *he* was already waiting for her with a hundred men-in-arms.

CHAPTER 5

Home

A S SOON AS she saw the first flash of sky blue and gold emblems from the old kingdom of Nor, Ameenah slowed Ifa's pace to give herself time to steady the pounding in her heart. There had never been any way to escape from him, despite the many times she had tried.

It hadn't been long since the last time they saw each other, so it vexed her even more that, despite the fact that she had known him all her life, time had done nothing to dampen his effect on her. It wasn't fair.

Though his eyes were several shades darker than hers, and hidden at this distance, Ameenah could still feel them boring into her skin from under his commanding brows. Through the trees, she could see that his arms were crossed over the crisp black folds of his tunic. The sapphire hilt of the kaskara at his back glinted in the sun as he waited near her front gate, flanked on either side by soldiers on horseback. *His* soldiers, the fiercest Simbu Ki in all five provinces.

As soon as Ifa broke through the tree line, Ameenah saw the smallest trace of a smile light up his beautiful face.

"Opa said that he expected you back last night. I had scouts looking for you on every route to and from Djobi. I'm glad to see you made it home safely."

"Nasir, what are you doing here?"

He waited until she dismounted, until he could see her stand on her own two feet before surrendering the last bit of tension in his body.

"Looking after you, of course." He didn't have to wait long for the scowl he knew was coming. Her thick curls rattled as she shook her head. How he'd missed that sound!

Ameenah turned from him, walking towards the wagon to unpack her things.

"I don't need you looking after me," she grumbled, reaching for her mirror and bag. She hadn't realized how close he was until he reached up behind her and lifted both things beyond her grasp. He moved so quickly that she had no hope of stopping him. In her distraction, he grabbed two more packages and walked away.

With an ease she was loathed to admire, Ameenah watched him balance his burdens while opening her gate and heading towards her front door.

"Will you just barge into my home then?" she asked, stopping him just as his hand rested on her door handle.

Nasir turned to her, eyes ever-earnest, ever-pure in his desire to help her, to love her. He had not changed since they were children.

I am a fool, she thought. They were surrounded by soldiers who had delayed their journey to go only the Mother knows where just to make sure she was safe, and they'd done so for no other reason than Nasir's command.

"May I come in, Ameenah?"

All her efforts to keep him away had never won an inch of ground. She could not rid herself of the only person in the world who truly knew her. He was the only living secret she had left to lose. She carried Nasir with her everywhere.

With silent resignation, Ameenah pushed the door open. Nasir walked inside and waited for her to come in and kick off her shoes in the haphazard way she always did. It was only after he closed the door behind them that she looked up to find him watching her. Just for a moment their eyes met and the rush of a thousand kisses they had never shared filled her as he leaned in and whispered, "I'm glad you're home."

He walked straight through her house, dropping her clothes at the back door where he knew she did her washing, then heading to her workshop where she made and stored her goods. Nasir knew his way around her home almost as well as she did. He'd helped her build it even as he'd tried to convince her not to live here. But as he went to place the mirror on the shelf where he last remembered it, Ameenah stopped him.

"No, no. It goes over there now." Ameenah circled the room to illustrate. "Everything's organized from left to right now. Raw material here, cured leather and woven things here, finished items, then supplies. See?"

Ameenah finished her demonstration only to find Nasir looking at her with the benign pity that polite people carried for the slightly insane.

"It's good to know you haven't changed. Still lining up your toys from smallest to largest," he teased.

It was a game she forced him to play when they were children. He called it stupid then, and it was clear his opinion had not improved.

"Oh, be quiet!" she snapped.

"Is that your way of saying, 'It's nice to see you, too Nasir. Thank you for helping me unload my things.'"

Ameenah's mouth hung open, stunned by her own rudeness.

"I'm sorry, Nasir," she stammered. "I do appreciate it. My manners are terrible."

Ameenah racked her brain to think of something she might say or do to make up for her awful behavior when she remembered the battered satchel Nasir had thrown away during his last visit.

"Oh! I do have something for you." Rushing to the shelf closest to her, Ameenah pulled a large brown bag from a basket.

"Here," she said, handing it to Nasir. "I fixed the handle on the satchel your mother gave you."

He barely recognized it as the same bag that had fallen from his saddle and been trampled on the road. The leather was glossy and supple as if it were brand new.

"Thank you," he replied as he looked for the place where the strap had torn from the bag. There was no indication of where she had patched it, only an intricate new design woven through the strap that somehow made it feel stronger.

With an awed smile, Nasir shook his head. "The harvest. Your work. This bag. Everything you touch is like magic."

"Only you think that," she replied.

"I'm sure there are others." His eyes on her were warm, searching. Ameenah had to look away.

"Can I offer you and your men some food, and water for their horses? I'm sure Opa has made bread, by now." Just then, the thing that had been missing since she arrived occurred to her.

"Where is Opa, anyway? He's usually here to meet me when I return?"

"We were up most of the night, I'm a bit ashamed to say, sharing news from the provinces and worrying about you. I know I shouldn't have kept an old man up past three in the morning, but he *feels* so much younger whenever I talk to him," Nasir replied with a shrug. "As soon as we heard you coming, he left to rest. He said he knew he could trust me to lend a hand until he woke up—a rare vote of confidence in these parts."

Ameenah narrowed her eyes. The smirk on Nasir's face was almost intolerable. In her mind, she could see Opa spying on them from some secret corner, laughing to himself at her awkwardness. Curiosity and revenge begged her to run off and look for him, but Ameenah refused to give him any more amusement at her expense.

"Well, I can make you all something if you give me a moment to—"

"It's all right," Nasir chuckled. "We can't stay. I've already sent most of our soldiers ahead to the north, but I wanted to check on you before I left and ask again for you to return with me to Nor."

"Nasir, I can't."

"It's not like before." Nasir walked close enough for his delicious scent of sandalwood and myrrh to permeate the space between them. "The rumors are real, Ameenah. There are men marauding in the west and in the north, taking lands, burning villages."

"They hurt people, Ameenah. They hurt women. They say it's just bandits, thieves from other lands, but I know the Hir is behind this. It might be blasphemy for me to say it, but I feel it, Ameenah. I know I'm not wrong."

Ameenah could see the fear in his eyes and now, close up, the shadow of circles underneath his eyes. He hadn't been sleeping. He was worried for more than just her.

Did he stay up all night, fearing the worst as he waited for me? she wondered. Absently, Ameenah let her hand rest on his chest as she stroked one of the thick dreadlocks that draped over his shoulder.

"I'm sorry I worried you. I stopped by Siama's to deliver some things I brought for her. She was anxious about the raiders, too. She asked me to spend the night, so I stayed."

"I know," Nasir replied, relishing the feel of her touch on his body.

"How?"

"When my men couldn't find you on the Merchant Road, I thought of Siama. I couldn't imagine you stopping anywhere else. Thank the Mother, I still remembered how to get there. When I saw Ifa tied to the tree outside Siama's cabin, I knew you were safe, so I returned here to wait for you."

Guilt washed over her as she realized Nasir *had* stayed up all night.

"Siama would have loved to see you. You should have stayed with us."

Nasir stepped closer with a doubtful look in his eye.

"Is that what you would have wanted, Ameenah?"

It wasn't hard for Ameenah to imagine the restless torture of fighting her desire as she slept on a mat next to him. She looked away.

"I would not have wanted you to risk yourself for me," she answered.

Nasir wrapped his arms gently around her waist.

"Come back to Nor. My sister, Kiva, will make sure you're safe until I return."

"There is no place safe, Nasir. You know that."

"There are safer places than here, Ameenah."

"I can look after myself," she answered. Her voice was gentle but firm.

"Ameenah, you don't have to be alone. You can start over. *We* can start over."

The mere thought of trying to recreate her life— again—sent a shiver down her spine. "How can you say that?" Ameenah replied as her body slipped out of his grasp.

"The Hir is alive. The man responsible for the death of my entire family is alive! If what you say is true, the war could be starting all over again and I can't, Nasir. I can't join this fight and lose everything again."

"Rahmeel and my father think there is still time for a diplomatic solution. They believe there's a chance we can avoid war."

Nasir's words hung between them like a veil of mist, not substantial enough to obscure, but still powerful enough to divide. With faces turned in opposite directions, Ameenah stared at the rows of supplies on her shelf, while Nasir shifted restlessly.

"Is that what you believe?" Ameenah asked. Nasir's expression twisted in frustration.

"No," he answered finally.

Ameenah knew he spoke the truth. The high commander of Nor's army wouldn't be headed north if he agreed with his family.

"You're too smart to believe their lies, Nasir. My parents believed they could reason with the Hir and now they're dead."

"You think staying out here at the edge of the Forbidden Forest will protect you? You're lying to yourself if you do. *You're* too smart for that, Meena."

"I have a life here," Ameenah replied.

"This is not life, Meena! Running from everything and everyone you know, everyone who makes you feel something—that isn't life. Being afraid to reach out to the people who love you, the people *you* love is not life."

"This is life," he said, closing the distance between them and bringing his lips to hers.

They had almost kissed many times, but in her fear, Ameenah had always shied away, and Nasir, in his faithfulness, had never tried to change her mind. This time Ameenah didn't have time to think, and she'd never been so glad for the reprieve. The unexpected impact of their lips together sent a ripple of warm pleasure through her. Even with no practice at all, she knew what she wanted from him, and she opened her mouth willingly to taste him and finally see if all her fantasies about what his lips on her would feel like were right.

The contrast between his arms around her, hard and unyielding, and the plump softness of his lips was thrilling. She could taste the mangoes he'd had for breakfast mixed with a tang of salt that made her thirsty. Greedily, she pulled him closer, trying to drink him whole because it was better, so much better than she'd ever dared to imagine.

Nasir broke away, pressing his forehead to hers as he cradled her face with trembling hands.

"I would do anything for you, Meena. Anything in my power. But I can't hide. I want to marry you and have children. I want to build a life worth fighting for, dying for, a life worth burning down this world to protect. But I can't hide anymore and neither can you. I feel it, Meena, and I know you do, too. We were meant for more than this. But you have to choose it, Meena. *You* have to choose it."

Ameenah pressed her fingers through his hands on her cheeks, trying to memorize the feel of his palms. All their years together as children, as friends, and much more than that, she had never allowed herself to be this close to him. Yet she could not meet his gaze. The truth of his words made her tremble. He had offered her his love and all the pieces that would make up their life, but her heart wasn't strong enough to hold them together.

"Ameenah, look at me," Nasir whispered.

Instead, she pressed her forehead closer, keeping her eyes tightly closed.

Though his heart broke to see her so conflicted, Nasir was not surprised. For years he had tried to pull her from the nightmare of losing her family. He had helped her build the life she wanted even when he disagreed with her choice and supported every decision she'd made, even when it took her farther away from where he wanted her most, safe within his city, safe within his arms. But despite the closeness they had developed and every inch of trust he'd gained on the way to loving her, he had failed.

He'd always admired her tenacity, the sheer force of will that shaped her into the woman who stood before him. Nasir had hoped that this ability she had to remake herself would eventually heal the wounds of her past, but now he knew the truth. Every choice she'd made was tied to the night her family died and her determination never to be that vulnerable again, even if it meant living her life alone, without anyone, without him.

"What more can I give?" Nasir whispered as he pulled his body from hers and walked away.

Except this.

As he paused at her front door, he turned back one last time.

"I love you, Meena," he whispered barely loud enough for her to hear. "With all that I am, I love you."

Ameenah cried then, not because he left, but because she did not even have the courage to say the words that would make him stay.

CHAPTER 6

The Forest's Edge

AMEENAH WATCHED HIM leave, unable to move herself from the place where they had finally come together and broken apart. Though he had left before, many times, it had never been like this. Never before had he made his intentions so clear and never had she felt so unable to meet them. In his absence, the sudden stillness felt crushing, an endless void echoing with all the things she'd failed to say.

Normally, after a trip from Djobi, Ameenah would have busied herself unpacking and rearranging her workroom, but Nasir and his men had completed most of those tasks already. All that remained was unbridling Ifa and washing her clothes. But after setting Ifa free to wander, Ameenah couldn't face the sorry bag of laundry that Nasir had left by the back porch where he knew she liked to sit and do her washing.

How many sunsets have we shared on that porch, she wondered.
Me washing and him rinsing, then hanging up my clothes to dry.

I want to make a life worth fighting for.

The loneliness formed a mean, hard lump in her throat as she remembered the kiss he had given her and how far away his lips were from her now. For several hours, Ameenah shuffled around on bare feet, trying to make use of her time while still feeling miserable. Nasir's visit had tugged on the frayed edges of her life, unraveling her peace of mind. That she could resent and cherish the effect he had on her disturbed Ameenah even more. Unable to stand the home that suddenly felt like a cage of her own making, Ameenah grabbed a worn shawl from her trunk of clothes and stepped outside.

Soothed by the feel of warm earth between her toes, she headed towards the fields. To her left was her home, a circular cottage with a round, pointed roof made of braided bamboo leaves and tiger grass tucked into the backdrop of the Forbidden Forest. The entire structure was built upon large grey stone blocks that kept the house dry when the rains flooded the fields. Small porches extended from both the front and back doors, with the rear steps leading to the water well and the five chickens she kept in a small wooden coop.

To her right was the herb garden, a small grove of trees just in front of Opa's cottage, made in the same fashion as her own, and the woods that led to the Eastern Road. Before her, the back fence marked the beginning of her crop fields, which spanned the entire length of her farm. The rows of plants were crowded with dark green collards, teff, corn, turnips, cabbage, carrots, and onions.

Above, the second sun had faded behind the trees. Soon she would give up her light to the first moon, then dusk would fold into nightfall.

He must have reached the Ghoven River by now, Ameenah guessed, as she replayed their conversation in her mind.

This is not life, Nasir had said.

Unbidden images of her childhood came to her. Running behind Rahmeel, Nasir, and her older brother, Haveer, her own laughter as she played, her hair tangled with twigs and dust, wild and free.

Looking back, she barely recognized the child she had been. Never would she have thought that someone who had known only happiness could bear such pain. Ameenah closed her eyes against the fading sun and marveled at how, after everything that happened, Nasir had managed to keep so much of himself intact.

At least he has his family, she thought. *I have no one.* Be even as she said it, she could not escape the images of Siama, Oorala, Opa, and Nasir from rushing to the forefront of her mind. Despite the distance at which she held them, they had all tried to love her. The ache in her heart widened.

"This is not helping!" She sighed.

To ground herself once more in the life she had, the life she had *chosen,* Ameenah began to walk the perimeter of her farm. She had timed her trip to Djobi to coincide with the coming of the harvest.

Tomorrow, the first of her hired farmhands would arrive to prepare the Moon Season's crops for picking. From the fullness of the leaves that covered the ground, she could tell the harvest would be plentiful, easily two times the yield of last year. Ameenah welcomed the distraction more than ever, the chance to exorcise the longing Nasir stirred in her with the sweat and strain of hard labor.

Gaining no relief from her wandering, Ameenah was about to head back to the house when a flash of tan fur at the end of a row of cabbage leaves caught her eye.

She turned to find the strange wolf that had crossed her path before staring at her.

"Hello there, little friend."

Ameenah and Opa had both seen the wolf at the edge of her land, but this was the first time the wolf had crossed over. Four weeks ago, Opa warned her that the wolf seemed to be getting bolder, but Ameenah was not worried. It was only men who scared her.

Despite what most people feared, Ameenah knew that most wild animals shied away from people. It was an impulse she understood well which made it all the more curious why this animal would defy its basic instincts.

Is he hurt? she wondered. *No*, Ameenah decided. His stance was strong, bold.

Drawn to the creature, Ameenah moved forward. The wolf lifted its muzzle as if to challenge her resolve, but he did not back away. Ameenah continued towards the beast, though she could not fathom why until she was directly in front of it. Slowly, she kneeled before the wolf until they were face-to-face, then held out her palm. After a sharp sniff, the wolf leaned forward, licked her hand, then darted into the Forbidden Forest. Without a thought, Ameenah followed it.

At night the cover of darkness made everything peaceful, a perfect place to hide. But by day a strange fog hovered in the branches as if the breath of the trees themselves lingered in the air.

Ameenah ran to catch up with the wolf, who turned only once to make sure that she was still behind him. She had almost closed the distance between them when the wolf disappeared behind a large acacia tree. She rounded the trunk but did not see the wolf. Instead, she found a child no more than two years old winding a twig through his fingers. He sat naked on a log, without a concern in the world.

Startled by her discovery and out of breath, Ameenah glared openly.

"It's rude to stare," the child said, looking up at her with sharp eyes.

Ameenah blinked in surprise at the maturity of his words. "What are you doing here? Are you lost?"

"You are in *my* woods. Shouldn't I be asking you that question?" The child's voice was not a child's voice at all, but low and raspy, like a hiss.

Ameenah did not answer. Her shock at finding the child was slowly subsiding, making room for her senses to prickle with a new awareness. She scanned the area. The grounds around the child were eerily pristine, with no sign of a gathering that would explain how he came to be here. It was almost as if he'd appeared out of thin air.

The hair on her arms stood up in warning as she took a step back. *Something is wrong here*, she thought. Before her the child smiled, a menacing, condescending sneer.

"Fine then. Talk to the wolf if you won't speak to me."

Suddenly, the wolf appeared at her side, nudging her right hand with his long, narrow muzzle. Ameenah looked down to find his golden eyes searching hers without a trace of fear or malice. Though the child was surely the rudest urchin she'd ever met, Ameenah could not find it in herself to fault the wolf.

Have you brought me here to rescue the child, she wondered silently as she rubbed behind his ear. The wolf leaned heavily into her thigh contentedly. She had no doubt that the creature had led her to this place, but she could not imagine that a child so small could have a beast as a pet, much less be able to control it enough to do his bidding.

In front of her, the child stared at the wolf and sucked his teeth.

"At least one of you knows who you are."

Confused, Ameenah looked from the wolf to the child.

"How could either of you know who I am?" Ameenah asked indignantly.

"I would not have wasted my time bringing you here if I didn't. The question is, why did you come if you do not know?"

Ameenah had no answer. Her mind was racing. *This is a child,* she thought. *No more. He couldn't know me.* But the words felt flimsy as they slipped from her mind.

"Does the forest not scare you, child?" the boy asked. "It is forbidden. Few would freely enter as far as you have come."

"The forest has never frightened me," Ameenah answered honestly.

"And why is that?"

"My mother used to bring me here," Ameenah replied. "Or someplace like it. She said the forest would never harm me."

"And do you know why this is true, or do you just believe everything your mother told you?"

Ameenah stiffened at the child's audacity, yet she still could not find the words to speak. With a sigh of exasperation, the child continued.

"I see. A mother's words are often enough for a child, I suppose. Would that your 'Ina' had told you more."

"You never knew my mother!" Ameenah snapped, angry at her mother's name in his mouth. "You're... a baby."

"If I'm a child, then you are less than that! You know nothing. Only your lineage protects you from your own ignorance. Why do you think your mother told you never to take off the necklace you wear? Are you so blind you only see what others tell you to see?"

Hurt, fear, and anger burned in Ameenah as tears welled in her eyes. She had been so focused on the child that she hadn't noticed the fog descend from the tree branches and billow out, surrounding them in a mist so dense that she could not tell where she was, or, more importantly, which way to go if she needed to escape.

But more than that, Ameenah was sure that the shawl around her shoulders and neck kept the coarse straps of her mother's necklace from view. Yet somehow the child knew. Ameenah reached for her dagger.

The child barked out a harsh laugh as Ameenah watched his eyes grow large.

Like an animal's, Ameenah thought.

"We feed on the stupidity of your kind," the child spat. "If I wanted anything from you I would have it by now."

Fed up with the child's foul words, Ameenah unsheathed her blade and took a fighting stance. If the child was a trap meant to lure her while others attacked, she would not be taken without a fight. Beside her, the wolf reached up to lick the hand that held the knife.

Stand with me or move away, Ameenah thought, as she tried to step away from the beast. But the wolf only drew closer, like a shadow.

In front of her, the child looked more annoyed than afraid as he continued.

"Look at it with new eyes before I lose my patience."

She did not need to ask what he meant. The necklace began to tingle and burn against her skin until she had no choice but to reach within the folds of her shawl and pull the necklace out.

She had worn it every day since her mother was taken. The necklace had been too big for her then, swinging uncomfortably against her diaphragm. But over the years she grew into it, cherishing it until she knew it as well as her own body.

By all accounts (even Ameenah's), it was an ugly thing, made of coarse, brown twine that had been worn down from constant wear and a jagged black rock that was twisted and intertwined within the rope. The necklace seemed completely out of place with the other pieces of fine jewelry her mother wore. Yet Fewa had given this specifically to her only daughter, making her promise never to take it off, and so Ameenah had not.

But now, as she brought it out into the fading light and fog of the forest, it changed. Through the mist that surrounded them, the coarse twine dissolved into a subtle woven link of gold, and the stone, which once had the look of coal, morphed into a smooth, translucent jewel with flecks of gold and pearl within its black depths.

The child in front of her gasped in awe.

"A true daughter of Amalaki," he whispered. "How long it has been?"

"What is this? How is this possible?" Ameenah stammered through her own disbelief.

"Your amulet possesses a powerful cloaking spell; its disguise protects its secrets from unfriendly eyes—the secrets of the Amasiti."

Ameenah frowned in confusion.

"The Amasiti are a legend," she murmured. "Nothing more."

The child looked at her with scorn. "You hold the proof in your hands! They are as real as your mother was—as *you* are!"

"What do you know of my mother? Tell me!"

But before he could answer, the child's head jerked back as if distracted by some sound Ameenah could not hear. Beside her, the wolf shifted from her side in a restless loop until he finally let out a piercing howl, then ran away.

"You must leave here!" The child's tone was tinged with annoyance. "There are more urgent matters to attend to."

"No! I need to know what this means. Why is there a spell on my mother's necklace? Who are you?"

The child ignored her as he threw down the twig he'd been playing with, then propelled his chubby legs to the ground with surprising ease.

"Leave," he snapped as he waddled away. Ameenah sheathed her dagger and caught up to him quickly, placing a hand on his shoulder with every intention of picking him up.

She had no idea.

The child whirled around, capturing her wrist with a lethal quickness. At first, Ameenah struggled to free herself from his unnatural grip, but then the child began to grow and change before her eyes. The toddler before her transformed into a creature with the torso of a man with horns protruding from his skull and the lower body of a gazelle. At eight feet tall, he towered over her. His sneer revealed a mouthful of narrow, sharp teeth.

"You will demand nothing from me!" he hissed before releasing her wrist. Ameenah staggered back as his front hooves stepped forward.

"You may have the blood, but you have none of the wisdom. You don't even know who you are!"

His four feet stomped the ground in front of him, resisting the urge to charge.

"There will be time enough to see if you are worthy of your kin, but for now, you must leave."

His nostrils flared, but Ameenah was relieved to see that his hooves retreated.

Truly terrified, Ameenah turned and ran through the mist, looking back only to make sure she was not followed.

CHAPTER 7

Unrest

AMEENAH STEPPED OUT from the tall trees of the forest into an uncertain hour. As soon as she passed through the lower saplings and brush that bordered her home, the fog behind her vanished. She could not say how long it took her to make it back. She had no sense of time or even distance. Her encounter in the woods had left her mind scattered.

Normally, she would have assumed that it was late, evening perhaps, but with both moons hidden behind low, heavy clouds, there was no way of knowing. Worse, the ground was wet from a recent rain, driving all the usual creatures that would have told her the hour into the warmth of their homes. But more than that, she sensed an unnatural stillness that only heightened her apprehension.

The walk back to the cottage was slow by necessity. Once the fear of imminent death subsided, Ameenah could barely get her legs to cooperate with the simplest of motions. She stumbled past the trees she had seen so many times before with brand-new understanding. There was magic, real magic, in the forest.

The Forbidden Forest had not been her first choice for a place to live. When it was clear to Siama that Ameenah had inherited her mother's talent for weaving, they talked about how she could master her craft and make a living for herself. It had not been Siama's intention to send her away. But after much begging and cajoling on Ameenah's part, Siama finally relented, allowing her to take an apprenticeship with Yeimi Attallah, the best tanner in Anam and a trusted friend of Siama's from since they were children. At the time, Ameenah was only a girl of twelve years old, but what she lacked in age she more than made up for in determination.

Ameenah surpassed the skill of her master in less than a year, then continued to apprentice with other fine artisans in basket-weaving and cloth-making. In addition to the money she earned working in their stores, Ameenah began selling her own creations. Shortly after, she started saving the proceeds to build her own workshop, where she would apply all the disciplines she had learned. By fifteen, Ameenah was anxious to strike out on her own, but reality proved harsher than she planned.

From the time Yet was established, land ownership was forbidden. It was the one rule that held true in all five kingdoms. In lieu of ownership, each citizen petitioned their province council for the right to become a land keeper with a parcel designated for his or her own use and purpose. Some citizens became land managers of larger parcels, offering cleared lands for rent.

But, a girl on her own with no family to vouch for her had little access to the reputable land keepers who promised cleared parcels at reasonable rates and guaranteed security. A girl on her own was not respectable and was therefore bound to cause trouble.

This left her at the mercy of more unscrupulous land keepers who sought to charge her twice as much as punishment for the scandalous nature of her circumstances. Fed up with being preyed upon, Ameenah sought her land claim farther out into the wild, where the share tax was cheaper and there would be no competition for her plot. Myths and legends had never bothered her. Having lost her family, she had already endured a cruelty far worse than any nightmare one could imagine.

When Ameenah first came to inspect the parcel that would become her farm, the surveyor told her of the strange creatures that lived in the Forbidden Forest. Fiendish beasts with razor-sharp teeth that ate animal and human alike. The Sri, the surveyor had called them, claiming that they had come into existence after the Fall of Elan as a curse from Amalaki for the destruction of the Amasiti.

Nonsense, she'd told him. Pure nonsense. Ameenah paid the surveyor handsomely for his bravery, sent him on his way, and never looked back.

Despite having made her home at the edge of a place most feared to tread, she had never witnessed anything that warranted the reexamination of her disbelief. For seven years, Ameenah worked to tame this happily-forgotten plot of land, shaping it to meet her needs and support her livelihood. Fear of the man-eating creatures kept most travelers away from the area, which suited Ameenah just fine. Now she knew how right they were and how arrogant she had been to ignore their warnings.

With the safety of her back porch in view, Ameenah clutched the cord around her neck and looked at it once again. Gone was the fine gold rope and the pearlescent stone wrapped in a delicate filigree of gold twine. Her necklace had returned to the way she'd always known it, unremarkable coarse rope wrapped around an ugly black stone.

This spell, this *thing*, was more than just a relic of her past. It held a deeper meaning for her mother, and perhaps for her. *I must know*, she thought.

Instinct mixed with pure longing wanted to draw her back to the forest, but her common sense—and the cuts packed with mud on the soles of her feet—knew better. They testified as to how far and how quickly they'd carried her to get away, and how painful a journey back might be.

Resigned to the reality that she must continue her inquiry another day, Ameenah climbed the stairs to her porch, pulled open the door, and stepped into the comfort of her kitchen. Despite the recent rains, the air inside was warm and dry, aided by a fire in the hearth that had only just died down.

Opa.

Ameenah smiled as she found him hunched over and snoring lightly at her kitchen table. Beside him was a plate of food covered by a heavy cloth to keep the flies away. Ameenah knew he had set it aside just for her.

It must be quite late, she realized. *How long was I in the forest?* What felt like minutes had clearly been much longer.

Carefully, Ameenah lifted the napkin. Injera, collard greens, and potatoes and onions. The smell made her mouth water as she smiled softly in gratitude. She could almost see his furrowed brow as he'd waited for her until the warmth of the fire finally lulled him to rest. After the evening she'd had, Ameenah was more sorry than ever to have missed their nightly dinner ritual. Still, if he had been awake, she wasn't sure what she would have told him about the things she'd experienced.

I barely understand it myself, she thought.

Too exhausted to wrestle with any more of her questions, Ameenah gently draped her shawl over him before grabbing a large bowl and soap from the washbasin to clean the cuts on her feet. With just enough light from the burning embers of the fire, Ameenah sat down and worked quickly to clean the wounds and treat them with a salve she made herself. By the time she was finished, Ameenah felt too tired to do anything but sleep. Opa's dinner would have to wait until morning.

Who knows how long I have till morning? Then, the harvest begins, she thought with a flash of irritation. Ameenah put the basin and soap aside and crept to her bed at the far end of the cottage.

Between brooding over Nasir and being chased by evil spirits in the forest, I've lost the whole day! she chided herself. *The moon harvest is in a few hours. I can't afford these distractions.* First and foremost, she had to ensure her own survival. Reluctant but resolved, Ameenah pulled the curtain that separated her bed from the main cottage and placed her blade on the stool beside her bed.

"First, the harvest, then I'll go back and make that *thing* tell me what he knows of my mother," she mumbled. Too tired to take off even a single item of clothing, Ameenah collapsed atop the bed, holding her mother's necklace until she fell asleep.

Two hours later, Ameenah jolted awake, startled by a large crash on the side of the house. Her first instinct was to dismiss it. Small animals were always foraging through the fields, she reasoned. One probably got entangled in a pile of wood and knocked it over. Ameenah was about to turn over in her bed and fight her way back to sleep when she heard the sound again, softer this time, but more distinct. She heard voices, strange and unrecognizable. Whatever was happening outside was still in play.

She rose from her bed, knife in hand and checked the kitchen, but Opa was gone. Silently, she hoped that he was fast asleep and undisturbed in his bed. Ameenah slipped into the darkness of her front parlor, grabbing her quiver of arrows and bow that rested by the door.

Peering through the large front window, she saw nothing. From the trees to the front gate to the garden, nothing was amiss. But then she heard it, a cruel laugh coming from the side of the house. Ameenah stepped forward, pressing her face to the window to understand the situation before she struck. From the far edge of the herb garden, she could see Opa with his hands raised high in supplication. Behind him stood a large burly man in dark clothing who taunted Opa while holding a large knife pressed against his throat. She closed her eyes and listened.

"Too bad you were up, old man. They told us the workers weren't expected 'til tomorrow. Can't have you screaming and ruining our fun, now, can we?"

"Please, we have nothing, only the harvest. How will we eat?"

Though the tension in Opa's voice was real, his tone was filled with something more than fear. Opa was a proud man and more capable than most men half his age. He would never give in so easily to a group of thieves. *No*, Ameenah realized. *He's buying us time.* She opened the front door slowly, holding it ajar with one foot so that she could set her bow. When she was ready, Ameenah released the door, letting it slam shut with just enough sound to catch the large man's attention and allow her to get in position to strike.

The man leaned his head back, just enough to elongate his throat, leaving it in full view. Crouched behind the front porch railing, Ameenah let her black-tipped arrow fly. He would never notice the sharp edge singing through the air until it sliced his throat. With a watery gasp, he fell to the dirt.

Keeping low to the ground, Ameenah rushed to Opa's side.

"Thank the Mother," Opa whispered, still trembling.

"Are you all right?" she asked.

Opa nodded, touching his throat gingerly. "Yes," he replied, "but you should run into the woods. I know these kinds of men, Ameenah. You must not be caught here."

Ameenah swallowed hard at the fear in Opa's words and the memory of what she knew the woods held for her. "How many?"

"Too many. Too many for us alone."

Ameenah nodded her understanding, but set her lips in determination and listened. There was no way she would leave Opa behind to face whatever threatened them. Slowly, her ears opened up and she could hear the tin of sharp blades ravaging the earth and the dull rhythm of feet carelessly stomping through tender soil. The chickens she kept for eggs made no sound; she knew they were dead already.

"Stay in the house!" she commanded. "Lock the door!"

Before Opa could grab her arm to hold her back, she was gone.

One of the first things Ameenah did when she began tilling the soil for her farm was plant trees. They served many purposes: to protect the land from erosion when the rains came and to keep her yields from any prying eyes that would seek to assess the fruits of her labor for their own gain, but that wasn't all. As she pulled her torso up and over a low but sturdy tree branch, Ameenah had never been so grateful for the last reason. She had wanted to plant sparrow trees because of the lush fruit and orange blossoms that cycled in and out of bloom twice each year. But Nasir had insisted on Kanfir trees instead.

"They grow quick and strong," he had explained. "Each branch is strong enough to hold a man's weight, while still providing enough leaves to camouflage an attack."

As Ameenah took an arrow from her quiver and aimed her bow, she could finally appreciate exactly what Nasir meant.

The rising of the first sun gave only the faintest shimmer of light against the dark clouds, but it was all the light her sharp eyes needed. To disguise her position for as long as possible, Ameenah aimed for the men in the fields first, firing four shots before anyone knew where they came from. Atop her perch, Ameenah counted more than a dozen men hacking their way through her fields, but once she began shooting them down, many scattered. She managed to kill five more before someone from below snuck up behind her. By the time Ameenah heard the branch creak with the extra weight and turned to aim, it was too late. His grip on her ankle was firm, and as he tugged, Ameenah went crashing to the muddy ground, knocking her bow and quiver out of reach.

For a moment her attacker just stood in disbelief at the woman who had killed nine of his men. Then, without a word, he lunged. Ameenah rolled away before he could get his hands on her and ran. With a new group of men blocking her way to the front entrance, she darted toward the back of the house, where two more men were waiting for her.

Don't panic. Think! she told herself as the realization that she was trapped sunk in.

The smell of filth and liquor was heavy on them as they approached, with untamed malice in their eyes.

"This is the one causing so much trouble?" a skinny man with short grey hair sneered. "We will teach you your place."

A bald man with a wide, nearly toothless smile walked beside him. "She's good with a bow, but I want to see if she can handle my arrow."

A chorus of laughter surrounded her.

"You will die trying," Ameenah spat as her fear ripened into a ferocious madness. She unsheathed the dagger at her waist, anxious to find out which of the men before her would taste her blade first.

The two men in front rushed forward, but as the bald man reached out, Opa sprang from the back porch rail, slamming a shovel into his skull. At her back, the man that had dragged her from the tree was within arm's reach. Ameenah whirled around and stabbed him through the heart. The force of her own blow pushed them both to the ground and she used their momentum to drive her knife deep into his chest.

Without another weapon, Ameenah had no choice but to pull the blade out. The task proved more difficult than she imagined as the layers of fat, muscle, and bone cemented the knife in place. Behind her, she could hear another clash erupting, but she didn't dare turn around without a weapon in hand. It took barely a moment to wrest the dagger from his chest, but it was a moment she could not afford. In her instant of delay, one of the remaining men came close enough to try to smother her in a bear grip, but Ameenah had already seen him coming out of the corner of her eye and shifted as soon as the blade was free.

Slashing through the air wildly, the sharp edge of her blade caught the man across his left eye and down the bridge of his nose. He backed away wailing as blood rushed down his face. A few feet away, Opa lay unmoving on the ground.

"Opa!" she screamed, already running towards him, but a sudden grip around her waist held her back. The smell of stale liquor on her captor's breathe made her stomach churn with disgust as two others pinned back her arms and forced the knife from her hand.

With no weapon and three men pulling her to the ground, Ameenah felt the fear she'd previously managed to keep at bay break loose, threatening to drown her alive, until she heard the howl of a single wolf.

For a moment everyone froze.

"What the hell was that?" the man behind her whispered. Though his voice trembled, his grip on Ameenah did not loosen.

"Let's get her inside," another replied. "I don't plan to be eaten alive out here in the middle of nowhere. We should have just stuck to the plan like we did in Pelet."

Yet, no one moved. The silence stretched on for so long that some started to think they'd imagined the animal's cry. Others began to mock the sound with fake howls of their own, creating such a ruckus that only Ameenah heard the snarls from the forest—the call to charge.

Suddenly, the wolves attacked, crashing into the men that surrounded her in a whirlwind of sharp teeth and tawny fur. The frenzy of the wolves' siege made it difficult to gauge their numbers, but there were dozens from what Ameenah could hear and see. The sound of snapping bones and desperate screams echoed in her ears.

Men ran from every hiding place, inside her home and out. Ameenah had not realized how out-numbered they were until then. Those who managed to escape the first wave of wolves scurried down the path to the Eastern Road, hoping to reach the cover of the trees and retrieve their horses.

But they did not make it that far.

As the pounding of horse hooves shook the ground beneath her, Ameenah crawled to where Opa lay still as stone and cradled him in her arms. In the chaos that surrounded them, she looked up to find another uninvited—but very welcomed—arrival: the 2nd Battalion of Nor's Simbu-Ki burst through the trees—two hundred strong, stomping and cutting down every fleeing bandit in their path.

CHAPTER 8

2nd Battalion

BY THE TIME the Simbu-Ki reached Ameenah's front fence, nearly fifty men lay dead, scattered between Ameenah and Opa's cottages, the fields, and the path to the Eastern Road. Shaken by the horror of what did happen—and what could have happened, Ameenah struggled to put on her bravest face as Kiva, commander of the Simbu-Ki's 2nd Battalion, and Nasir's only sister, dismounted from her horse and ran toward her.

"Sister, are you hurt?" Kiva asked as she looked from Ameenah to Opa on the ground.

At first, Ameenah could not find her voice. Tears of relief welled up in her eyes.

"Ameenah," Kiva tried again, kneeling to hug her shoulders with one arm while checking Opa's pulse with the other. "Answer me!"

"I'm all right," she managed.

Kiva was far from convinced as she drew Ameenah more fully into her embrace.

"But Opa. He hasn't moved."

Kiva turned to her troops and shouted, "Abet, come! See to this man's injuries." A bald older man with a close-cropped salt-and-pepper beard ran towards them with a lantern in his hand. The saddlebag at his hip rattled with vials of healing ointments, bandages, and roots that could ease the worst pains.

"I'm sorry we didn't get here sooner," Kiva added as she watched. Abet knelt in front of Opa and begin checking his forehead and eyes for signs of injury.

"Bring the stretcher," Abet called, anticipating the sound of feet rushing to his aid. Instead, his request was met with silence. Confused, Abet tore his attention away from Opa and found his assistants standing at Ameenah's fence with the still-folded cot in their hands and terror in their eyes. They would not come closer.

Beside Abet, Kiva's voice was sharp as she addressed the men assigned to Abet's command. "Why do you linger?" she demanded, but her voice trailed off as she followed their gaze. Slowly, Kiva released Ameenah's shoulder and stood, edging her hands towards the sword at her hip.

"Ameenah," she whispered as a lone wolf advanced in front of the largest wolf pack Kiva had ever seen.

"Get behind me, then run when I tell you. The wolves have come to feed."

Behind her, Kiva's men dismounted from their horses and got in position to defend their commander.

Finally snapping out of her daze, Ameenah's hand rose to stay Kiva's sword.

"No. They have already fed. They are the reason we're still alive."

Confused, Kiva took a tiny step away as Ameenah rested Opa's head in Abet's hands then stood. The leader of the wolf pack trotted forward, sliding his narrow head underneath Ameenah's outstretched fingers. Ameenah knew him as the same wolf who had led her into the forest. Slowly, she knelt down to face him. Nothing about the wolf or the simmering pack behind him gave her pause as she gently stroked the path from his ear to his shoulder.

"Thank you, my friend. I owe you my life."

The wolf stepped deeper into Ameenah's embrace before resting back on its haunches and bowing low on his front legs. Kiva's soft gasp echoed behind her as the wolf lifted his head and howled. Behind him, the pack answered in a primal chorus that shook the leaves. When they were quiet once more, the lead wolf nodded its head towards Ameenah, holding her gaze for a brief moment before sprinting away and leading his pack back into the forest.

Opa regained consciousness shortly after the wolves left, allowing Abet to treat his wounds more thoroughly. After they settled Opa in his bed to rest, Ameenah and Kiva walked through the farm, assessing the damage the bandits had wrought as the first hired hands of the harvest crew arrived. Though the raider's brutal hands had ruined some of the crops, most of the harvest was hardy enough to survive.

"You have done well, sister. When my brother told me where you decided to settle, I feared neither of you would survive."

"How do you mean?" Ameenah frowned. "Nasir does not stay here."

"That's exactly what I mean. I feared that you would be over-come by the terrors of the Forbidden Forest and my brother would die from worry over you."

Ameenah turned away from Kiva's knowing gaze.

"He needn't worry," Ameenah mumbled as she bent down to pick up a fragment of fence that had been torn down in the bandits' frantic effort to flee the wolves. "I can take care of myself."

Kiva narrowed her eyes incredulously as Ameenah studiously avoided her gaze. Knowing that Nasir's sister would never back down, she sighed with resignation before finally meeting Kiva's stare.

"Clearly," Kiva replied, gesturing to the mayhem around them.

"It was safe. It had been before now," Ameenah protested.

Kiva scanned the chaos around them. Shards of broken glass from the windows were everywhere, and the doors were barely clinging to their hinges. Scattered farm tools, splintered barrels, and ruined pottery littered the entire area around Ameenah's home. In the fields, dozens of crops ripped from the ground lay wasting away. But that was not the worst of it.

Kiva's soldiers worked quickly to gather the dead and burn them away from Ameenah's sight, but the evidence of the carnage of the wolves was everywhere, staining the earth red. Kiva had seen similar bloodshed in every village the bandits attacked. The only difference this time was who lay dead.

Ameenah's home may have been a place of peace before, but now it has been marked. If they found her once, they can find her again. She must know this, Kiva thought. *Next time...*

Kiva shook her head to stop herself from completing the thought, her expression a mixture of sadness and anger.

"It must have been beautiful living here, hidden away from everyone and everything. But that time is over, Ameenah. You cannot be so naive if you hope to survive."

"I've traveled to Djobi and back by myself many times. If I were as naive as you think, I would never have survived such a trip."

"And how many raided villages did you pass along the way? How many hungry faces did you count on your travels? Did you even stop to see their suffering? Or did you hurry on your way, as if you are the only one who matters?"

Ameenah fell silent as guilt washed over her. She had always kept far away from the towns, keeping herself safe while ignoring the stories and plights of others.

"I don't mean to be harsh." But seeing the look on Ameenah's face, Kiva knew the damage had already been done. Silently, Kiva cursed herself. Whenever she was afraid, her instinct was always to lash out. She was still learning that fear was not always a foe to be slain. Kiva took a deep breath and tried again.

"I'm not saying it's your fault." Kiva paused, suddenly struck by the irony. "In a way, your home saved many people."

Ameenah looked back at Kiva, feeling unworthy of any reprieve from the guilt she now felt.

"How could that be possible? I've done nothing."

"I was meant to be with Nasir in the north. I met him at the Ghoven River after he left here. But instead of carrying on with him, he sent me back. He was worried that with so many of our forces in the north, protection of our own lands might be compromised. Since he had just patrolled the western border on his way to you, I decided to follow the river east, which is how we came across the raid in Pelet. When I saw what they did there, I knew we needed to check on you. Who knows how many others lives they might have destroyed if you and your wolves had not stopped them here?"

A shudder ran through Ameenah's body as the terror of what had happened just a few hours ago came back to her, the moment of helplessness before Kiva and the wolves arrived. She would not wish what she'd experienced on anyone.

Ameenah nodded then, grateful for the notion that she might have spared someone else from suffering her fate.

"I will have to tell Nasir that he needn't worry anymore. You have your own army," Kiva added.

Ameenah turned to the edge of the forest where her saviors had disappeared.

"The wolves," she whispered.

"Do you know why they came?" Kiva asked. "Their leader seemed to know you."

Immediately, Ameenah thought of the woods and the strange creature she encountered there, but nothing in her memory led to any answers.

"He's passed near the farm a few times over the years, but nothing like this has ever happened before."

Kiva studied Ameenah carefully, noting the haunted look in her eyes as she fingered the strange stone that hung at her neck. In that moment, Kiva knew there was more to the mystery of the wolves than mere coincidence, but she also sensed that the answers to her questions would not reveal themselves easily. When it became clear that Ameenah had no more insight to offer, Kiva broke the silence that had fallen between them.

"Well, whatever the reason, I'm glad of it. I am grateful to them for saving my sister's life."

Ameenah looked back at Kiva with a cautious smile.

"Thank you, sister!"

"I must report this raid to my father and Rahmeel in the capital, then we will continue our patrol of the area. Will you be all right on your own? I could leave some of my men."

"No. I'll be fine. Most of the harvest crew will be here is a few hours. I even hired a few more than usual just to cover the surplus I was expecting. I promise I can manage."

Kiva looked around, counting the men and women who now worked in every corner of Ameenah's farm. They were strong, wielding axes and machetes with ease. *Another small army if need be,* Kiva thought before turning back to Ameenah.

"All right then. Send word if you need anything."

"I will," Ameenah promised with more confidence than she felt. Kiva was not fooled.

"The power of the Hir is growing, Ameenah. You cannot simply hide yourself away here. We must come together if we hope to protect our way of life."

"Your brother said as much. You sound just like him," Ameenah replied.

"It is not only love, but truth that makes him say these things. You would do well to listen."

CHAPTER 9

The Moon Harvest

AMEENAH ALONG WITH all the farmhands she'd hired worked through the morning and well into the rise of the second moon. The adrenaline from the attack carried her through the day with a feverish energy until she collapsed in her bed that evening.

She woke up twice during the night, haunted by dreams of death closing in around her, only to be lulled back to sleep by the distant sound of wolves howling deep in the shadows of the forest.

But while the sounds of the wolves had brought Ameenah a sense of peace, the opposite seemed to be true of everyone else in the camp.

"Did you hear them last night? Like demons from the mouth of hell," Opa complained as he dragged a bag of split peas behind him in preparation for the breakfast. "I feared that we would wake up to find half our workers gone from fright."

"Those wolves saved our lives," she answered softly, adding chopped onions to the pan heating on the fire.

"Yes, they did," Opa replied with a shiver. He had been unconscious when the wolves arrived, but when he woke up, the evidence of their presence was clear enough to prove that the tales from Abet of their numbers and ferocity had not been exaggerated. He set the sack down beside the fire with a wince and headed toward the cutting table.

"I'm surprised to see you up so early. How are you feeling?" When he didn't answer right away, Ameenah looked up from her cooking to find Opa's face drawn and sweaty with pain.

"Opa," she sighed, walking over to take the knife from the injured hand he was stubbornly using to cut yesterday's injera into smaller pieces. "Forgive me. You should go back to bed and rest. I can prepare breakfast for the crew."

Relief flooded his sweat-slicked face, but still, he worried.

"We have more than two dozen workers. How will you manage on your own?"

"When the food comes too slowly for their liking, someone will come to help me." She smiled. "Please rest. If you're sick, who will barter for me when the trader's suppliers come?"

Opa shook his head with a knowing grin. Ameenah had no patience for bargaining. In Djobi, she was used to simply naming her price, take it or leave it. He marveled at how she managed to sell all of her wares every year with such blunt tactics.

"Yes, I suppose you're right. They will be here soon enough and one of us will need the strength to deal with them."

"Better you than me," she teased, leading him down the back steps and onto the path to his home at the eastern edge of the farm. Opa leaned heavily on his left side despite his best efforts to hide his pain, and Ameenah slowed her stride to hold him up more carefully.

After reaching his home and putting him to bed with food and water within reach, Ameenah covered Opa with one of the thick wool blankets she'd bought for him from Djobi two seasons ago.

"Is there anything else I can get you before I leave?"

"Go, child. The workers will want their breakfast soon. I just need a bit more rest," he mumbled, already overcome with exhaustion. Knowing he spoke the truth, Ameenah kissed him lightly on his forehead before closing the front door firmly behind her and rushing back to the kitchen.

With the crops proving more plentiful than even Ameenah had estimated, they worked from first sun to the rise of the second moon for three days straight. With the added work required to repair the damage left by the bandits, their workdays often extended even farther into the night. Each farmhand more than earned their daily allotment of provisions, which included a basket filled with injera, root vegetables, a head of cabbage, and three yams, in addition to the generous wages paid to those willing to work for the strange woman who lived at the edge of the Forbidden Forest.

She had worked with the same group of people for five seasons, culling and pruning their ranks until she knew and trusted almost every person who worked for her. The added familiarity helped, given Ameenah's meticulous standards for how her crops were harvested, prepared, and packed for the market. After so many seasons together, they knew what she and Opa expected of them, and they performed their tasks with minimal supervision or corrections.

Ameenah used a special washing solution for her vegetables that enhanced their flavor and kept them fresh on their journey to the markets throughout Yet. Nothing was rushed in the process, from picking to washing then drying and packing each vegetable, root, or fruit. And in so doing, Ameenah ensured her produce always fetched the highest price.

By the morning of the fifth day, more than half her crew had already begun the long journey back to their homes. The mending of her front fence was still far from complete, but most of the havoc wrought by the bandits had been repaired. Though some of the farmhands lingered to complete odd projects, Ameenah felt herself finally relaxing into the knowledge that the chaos and bustle of the past two weeks would soon be behind her. She could taste the craving for solitude on her tongue like the bite of bitter herbs. Her eyes burned to find empty space. Her ears ached for the blissful sound of utter silence.

Almost, she sighed. Almost.

Opa had made all the arrangements weeks ago. The first of the towns' suppliers from Nor would arrive before the rise of the second sun. By the end of the day, suppliers from Mir, Anam, and Kiveer would squabble over whatever produce Nor had left behind.

And then, it will be over, she told herself.

Opa was already perched against the newest section of the front fence, ordering various helpers this way and that to ensure that the produce carts were lined up far enough away from the area the builders needed to store supplies and cut the new fence.

Deciding that Opa appeared to have enough help at his side, Ameenah returned to the house. With any luck, she hoped to stay there all day, out of sight, until there was barely anyone left to see her.

Retreating farther into the safe cocoon of her workroom, Ameenah was already planning the intricate projects and orders that would fill her days in the months to come. She sat at her work table and pulled her sketching board from the table's side drawer. With charcoal in hand, Ameenah lost herself in sketching out requests from Djobi and new designs for her customers. Sometime later, she heard the approach of horses but ignored it. In her workshop, it was easy to block out every distraction from the outside world, which is why she didn't heed the sound of danger coming quickly to her doorstep.

Opa noticed it first: a stampede of large horses followed by the distinct timbre of a bell only used by the highest members of Yet's nobility. His first thought was of Nasir, but he had not been seen for weeks and Kiva had left only a few short days before. *No*, he thought, *this is something else.*

The first rider came tearing through the eastern path then, in a move clearly meant to intimidate, he stopped his horse only inches from where Opa stood. But, Opa stood tall. Shoulders squared, he looked past the billowing red drapery of the rider's clothes, the steel of his massive sword, and the gleam of his blackened armor to meet the man's eyes far above him.

"You there! Is this your property?"

"Who asks?" Opa replied, decidedly unimpressed with the man and his lack of manners.

"Gedeyon, of the Hir's personal guard," the man huffed from atop his seat. "Are you too simple to recognize the crest of the Hir?"

Opa's gaze meandered down to the blood-red sash that hung over the front of Gedeyon's saddle. Of course he'd seen the crest. It was just as ugly as he remembered it, a gold island being choked by a snake as it drowned in a blood-red sea. Thanks to the height of Gedeyon's horse, it stood right next to his face, but Opa needed to stall.

As far as he knew, the Hir's men had never come this close to the Forbidden Forest. No one came here unless they were paid well or lost. Opa felt sure that the Hir's men were neither. In fact, from Gedeyon's question, Opa suspected that he had come this way on purpose, looking for something or someone. Before Opa would answer, he wanted to know why.

"Yes, there it is," Opa replied lazily. Gedeyon bristled at Opa's blatant disregard.

"You should know it well, old man! The Hir keeps the way of this land and you would do well to honor it."

"Lots of ways to go these days, it seems. This way. That way. That path," Opa said pointing to the Eastern Road, "will take you all the way to Djobi, if you're lost."

"We do not seek that sinner's den," the guard scoffed. "I've come on the Hir's purpose!" The man reached into a leather satchel that hung off his red saddle. "We seek the—" He stopped abruptly as a voice rang out from behind the trees on the Eastern Road.

"Gedeyon! Why do you linger in this cursed place? No one with sense would choose to live here." The Hir's voice faded away as he cleared the trees and caught sight of the small farm before him.

The Hir rode forward in utter shock before his eyes caught Opa's and hid his emotions behind a more neutral façade.

"Forgive me, Ja Hir. This old man distracted me. I was about to tell him."

"Patience, Gedeyon," the Hir chided as he rode up beside them. "We must respect even the very old among us. For they too can often be of use." Five guards flanked him on each side.

Opa gaped at the man draped in red and gold before him, too frightened to move, as the Hir rode his great stallion toward Opa with casual superiority.

"Do not be afraid, Abati. Blessings to you and all those you hold dear." The Hir smiled as his black eyes flickered over the farmhands who gazed at him in awe.

"We only seek water for our horses. I am traveling the countryside to ensure all is well with our people," the Hir assured the small group before looking down at Opa with a smile that was sweet enough to rot anything it touched.

But Opa could barely make out the Hir's words over the sound of hissing in his ears. He stepped back, realization coming to him slowly as he watched the Hir's eyes comb through the collection of workers behind him with an intensity that was more than curiosity.

We've done nothing wrong, he tried to assure himself, but nothing would settle the sense of foreboding in his bones. *I must get him out of here as quickly as possible.*

"Of course, Ja Hir! Of course," he replied, recovering himself as he moved around the guard's horse. "We have fresh water just here." He motioned to the large trough Ameenah had installed by the front gate to make collecting water and serving Ifa easier.

"We are in your debt, Abati." The Hir motioned for his guards to move towards the basin while he kept his gaze on Opa.

"It is unusual to live so far away from the nearest town, but I see you manage well. Your harvest looks plentiful."

"Yes, Ja Hir. The Mother has blessed," Opa replied.

"And you manage here alone," the Hir inquired. Slowly, the Hir trotted his horse over the lines of harvest containers as if inspecting them carefully.

"Hardly alone, Ja Hir. It takes many to produce such good work."

"So I see," the Hir replied. The look on his face reeked of dissatisfaction as if Opa had given the wrong answer to his question.

"But all these good works mean nothing without a family to share it with. Have you no family, Abati? No one to care for you in your old age?"

A rush of heat jolted through Opa's skin as he finally realized who the Hir was looking for.

Just then, as if someone had called her by name, Ameenah appeared on her front porch.

The Hir looked up, meeting her eyes with a crazed gleam and a smile that was both sly and feral.

At first, Ameenah did not see him. She'd only come outside to find out if Nor's supplier had arrived and if so, gauge the state of negotiations. She cast another approving glance at the fine repairs to the back gate before turning towards the front of the farm. There she found a tall, thin man mounted on a horse that was far too large for the slight burden it carried. The man hid his fragile frame well behind the layers of red and black fabric, tucked and folded to make him appear larger than he was. Though his face was smooth, his eyes were squinted inside a face that was sharp and hollow. The hard bones betrayed the meanness of this spirit, and that was all Ameenah needed to see.

Her eyes dropped down to the sash that carried the crest of the Hir on his saddle.

What are the Hir's men doing here, she wondered. Ameenah's heart began to race inside her chest, but she told herself they had nothing to fear. *We have committed no offense.*

Beside the man on horseback, Ameenah noted that Opa's expression was tight with terror. His eyes bulged in their smooth brown sockets, willing her to run back into the house. But Ameenah did not understand until she saw the ring made of thick, black metal on the man's right hand. The blood-red jewel of the Hir drank in the light from the afternoon sun as if it was on fire. Now she understood the threat before them for exactly what it was. Ameenah did not know much about the Hir except that he was cruel. The fact that no one here had given him any cause to be so gave her no comfort at all.

You can't hide here, Kiva had warned her. *Not anymore.*

Slowly Ameenah stepped down from the porch, trying to remember her manners, her pleasantries, and anything else she could use to save those around her from the man who stood at her gate. The weight of their lives in her hands made her legs weak, but her countenance held firm as she racked her brain for the right words to keep them all alive. With no preparation and no clue as to how to manage the situation, the words that finally came to her were not her own.

"Ja Hir, you honor us with your presence. What assistance can we provide to The Keeper of Yet?"

The Hir let out a sound like a purr as he dismounted from his horse and walked towards her.

"It is I who should seek to serve you, my dear. I never imagined such a treasure could be found within the thorns of this treacherous forest."

Ameenah cast her eyes down to hide her disgust. By the time he spoke again, the Hir was close enough that she could smell the hearth-smoke and perfume on his clothes.

"I see I've made you uncomfortable. I beg your forgiveness," he continued in a voice that sounded all too self-satisfied. "May I be so bold as to ask your name and how you came to be in such a place?"

It took all her strength to meet his gaze.

"My name is Ameenah and this farm is my home, Ja Hir." Her words seem to stun him completely. He looked around at the workers, the old man he first encountered who now stared at him with open suspicion, then back to Ameenah.

"*Your* farm, you say? Surely you do not stay here alone?"

Ameenah hoped desperately that there was no trace of fear in her voice.

"I am not alone, Ja Hir," she answered with a shake of her head. While the sound of the tinkling bells in her hair comforted her, she noticed that the Hir stepped back with a slight cringe. Grateful for the new distance between them, Ameenah continued.

"My men are with me. Opa, whom I believe you've met, and many others."

Something in the way she stood apart made the Hir doubtful. As he looked beyond her, he noticed the signs of damage to the front gate.

"What happened here?"

Ameenah followed the direction of his gaze and winced. Unaccustomed to lying, Ameenah could only respond with the truth.

"We were attacked by bandits five days ago."

"It grieves me to hear it. I hope you weren't too badly hurt?"

"No, Ja Hir. You misunderstand me. The bandits came, but they did not get what they came for." Rather than relief, the Hir's expression was more akin to surprise.

"How do you mean?" His voice was sharp with disbelief.

"They are dead, Ja Hir."

"All of them?!"

Ameenah narrowed her eyes. "Did you know them, Ja Hir, the men who attacked my home?"

The Hir stiffened.

"Only by reputation. My men and I have been tracking their movements, but the criminals have managed to escape our group. Though I am glad to hear of their demise, I wonder how so few of you were able to defeat so many. From the reports I've been given the ruffians travel in groups of forty men or more."

"The forces of Nor came to our aid, Ja Hir. They are the ones who deserve credit for our safety."

The Hir looked away, pondering something that seemed to cause him great distress.

"I see," he murmured. "I will be sure to take note of that." His tone made Ameenah glad she did not mention Kiva by name.

"At any rate, it would please me to offer the services of my men to protect your… *home* against any dangers that may return. You can never be too careful."

"Thank you for your generosity, Ja Hir, but others need protection more than I."

"Yes," he replied, stepping towards her again. "But none deserve it more than you." His gaze lingered over her body like a slimy film that would not easily be washed away.

When his hand reached out to touch her shoulder, a wind picked up around them, rattling the leaves and tossing her hair so the bells and trinkets within it let out a shimmering sound.

The Hir recoiled as if his hand was singed by fire. In an effort to keep his reaction from her, he turned to mount his horse, retreating from her entirely. As briskly as it came, the air settled around them again, leaving everything quiet once more. With a flick of his wrist, most of his guards headed back toward the Eastern Road.

In the renewed silence, the Hir once again adopted his veneer of goodwill as he bowed to Ameenah.

"My offer still stands," he said. "You are noble to think of others, my dear, but my protection is yours should you need it. You are either the hunter or the hunted. And few get to choose which one they will be."

Ameenah held her tongue, instead using all her energy to silently will him away.

The Hir tilted his head with a pensive gaze before turning away and riding out with the rest of his guard. Ameenah stood watching the path he took for some time as those around her hurried to complete their tasks and head home. Silently, she prayed that somehow the whole strange incident had been resolved, with no chance that their paths would ever cross again. But the growing dread in her heart and the howl of a lone wolf in the forest told the truth: that whatever had been set in motion by his visit had only just begun.

CHAPTER 10

An Uneasy Pair

IT BEGAN IN the town of Riva, which sat just north of the border between Nor and Anam. At just over fifty miles away, it was also the closest town to Ameenah's farm.

The first soldiers arrived with much fanfare, announcing a new decree from the Hir that promised an end to the looting that plagued Yet. Initially, people believed the Hir's only intention was to increase patrols in the area. After years of neglect, it didn't occur to them to expect more. So when the next wave of soldiers came with food and supplies to restore the grain and repair the damage left by the bandits, no one had any idea what to make of it.

By in large, initial reactions were skeptical. The Hir's disinterest in the troubles of common people was well-known. But as the weeks went on, and the provisions and lumber kept coming, cynicism gave way to acceptance and gratitude as the people of Riva began to feel safe in their homes once more. Then, when all their basic needs were met, gratitude turned into curiosity about the reason for the Hir's sudden interest in their well-being. *Why now? Why Riva?* they wondered.

The answer came from the mouths of the Hir's own soldiers, tales of a young woman who lived at the edge of the Forbidden Forest. The soldiers told of her uncommon beauty and how she had captured the heart of the Hir.

"She and her home had nearly been ravaged by the same bandits who marauded from town to town," they said. "Until the noble Hir and his men arrived in the nick of time to rescue her from certain death!"

So taken was the Hir with this mysterious woman that her predicament opened his heart once more to the plight of his people. Because of her, the soldiers said, the Hir had committed himself to a benevolent rule once more. It did not take long for those from Riva who had bartered with Ameenah on one of her rare trips to recall the strange, reclusive girl and spread the tale of her encounter with the Hir to anyone who would listen.

After weeks of no word from or sight of the Hir and his men, Ameenah was beginning to hope that her instincts had been wrong and that somehow, she had managed to slip out of the Hir's mind. It was only when Opa returned from an impromptu trip to Riva for supplies that she learned just how wrong she had been.

Having heard his approach on the road, Ameenah hung the last of their laundry on the clothesline then walked to the front gate. She was hopeful that Opa had been able to locate the solvent she needed to prepare the hides she had just cleaned for stretching.

Though the concoction was simple to make, it took time, time that Ameenah had lost in tending to the repairs. The solvent from Riva would serve as a good base on which to build her own special blend to treat the hides, making them both unusually supple and strong. But as he emerged from the trees, Ameenah saw the hard lines etched across Opa's face and began to worry that the usual makers she preferred had been out of the supplies she needed.

"Opa, what is it? Did the trip not go well?"

Opa's frown only deepened as his lithe body slid down from his saddle with ease.

At least he's not hurt, she thought, grateful for how quickly Opa had healed from the attack.

When he still did not answer her query, Ameenah followed him in silence. Opa walked to the wagon behind Ifa and began untying packages. Though Opa was often quiet, he was never rude. Everything he did had a purpose. The fact that Opa had not answered her question was telling. Something on his trip had disturbed him greatly and if he would not speak of it, Ameenah knew it was because the matter was still not resolved in his mind. She would not ask him again.

They worked together, unbundling packages and sorting the delicate items that would need to be carried with care.

"It appears you are quite famous," he said finally. "Compliments of the Hir."

At the mention of his name, Ameenah nearly dropped the glass jar of solvent that she'd been holding.

"What?" She found herself unable to think or say more.

"It appears that the Hir has been using the story of the raid on your home to gain sympathies. The people of Riva believe the Hir to be a Great Hero. He saved your life."

"That's nonsense! He wasn't even here."

"No, he wasn't. A fact I conveyed to anyone who cared to hear it."

"And?"

"With their bellies full and their roofs fixed, no one cared."

The lines on Opa's face grew darker as he lifted a bag of lentils in his arms and headed towards the house. Ameenah grabbed the second bag and followed him.

"What do you mean, no one cared to listen? He had nothing to do with it."

Opa dropped the bag on the kitchen floor, then turned to cut her off.

"Ameenah, none of this matters! The truth. Your word. None of it. Before you left for Djobi, every man secretly cursed the name of the Hir. Now, you should hear them! Falling like sycophants over his every gesture.

"He's been giving them food, supplies, and clothing for weeks. His guards patrol their streets unchallenged. In fact, the people welcome them as saviors." Opa's eyes were wide with disbelief as he sighed and shook his head. "There hasn't been a raid in weeks. That is all they care about."

Abruptly, Opa walked back to the wagon. Though his demeanor was sharp with frustration, Ameenah knew that he was not angry with her.

"But what does any of that have to do with me?" she asked, trailing behind him. Her voice faded as Opa reached into the satchel that was slung over Ifa's side, pulled out a rolled length of finely-woven cotton and handed it to her. Confused, Ameenah looked at the fabric and wondered why Opa would have bought something so costly when it was not on their list of supplies.

"A gift from the people of Riva," he explained.

Ameenah stared back at Opa blankly.

"For opening the Hir's heart to his people."

Ameenah dropped the package on the floor and backed away as if a viper had slithered out to bite her.

"I did nothing," she whispered. Her stomach felt queasy.

Opa nodded before bending down to pick up the package.

"Indeed," he replied, placing the fabric back in her arms. "And yet, this is the story being told. A young girl alone in the forest, rescued by the noble Hir. A beautiful girl awakening the passion of a ruler for his people."

Ameenah shrunk from the meaning behind Opa's words.

"But why, Opa? Why would they spread these lies?"

"I don't know, Ameenah. But he will be here in three days."

In the weeks that followed, Ameenah would come to look at the month-long reprieve from the Hir's presence as a gift she could not fully appreciate until it was gone. The second time he came, he brought with him a full retinue of guards and dignitaries, along with what seemed to Ameenah to be half the town of Riva.

Of course, all of them had not been summoned to the visit. Most came purely out of curiosity to see with their own eyes the woman who had finally captured the Hir's affection. Ameenah tried her best to appear grateful for his generosity to Riva while never giving away anything that could be construed as encouragement of his advances. But it did not work. The more she withdrew herself from him, the more frequent his visits became.

Any excuse to visit would suffice. Whether stopping by to water his horses or to inquire about her safety, he came repeatedly and unannounced. Once, to pass the awkward moments between them as he drilled her with questions about how she made her living, she offered to show him her farm. They'd walked only a short distance around the perimeter before he seemed thoroughly bored. Afterwards, he offered a thinly-veiled excuse to leave. Ameenah had been only too happy to bid him farewell.

To her relief, he never expressed any interest in entering her home. And she never offered. Her private home was sacred to her, filled with the last remnants and precious belongings of her family. If suffering through these brief but awkward moments were all she would have to endure to help the people of Riva, she would bear it gladly. But that was not all that some required of her.

In between these visits, people from Riva and other villages who were now benefitting from the Hir's generosity began to call on her, singing the Hir's praises and encouraging her to accept his advances as a means of securing their own survival.

Ameenah was happy for any relief that came to the people of Yet, though she seriously doubted she'd played any role in easing their struggles. But, if something she'd done unwittingly could have opened the Hir's heart to his people, shouldn't she be glad? Her mind said yes, but her heart—and the look in Opa's eyes— told her everything was not as it seemed. Inside, Ameenah knew that with every visit, something was building, something she did not want, but could not stop.

At first it was just the merchants and farmers from nearby towns and villages. Having lived similar lives of independent solitude, these were the easiest people to turn away. Though they enjoyed the new prosperity that came with the Hir's favor, they also valued their freedom, and would not trade it easily.

"You are blessed," a young mother said, carrying her newborn child on her back. She was the first to arrive, bringing a gourd of her best palm oil to thank Ameenah for encouraging the Hir to help her village.

"I did nothing," Ameenah protested, insisting that the woman keep her gift. "I do not deserve your offering. I did not ask the Hir to come. I did not want him to come."

"Just because you do not intend to be a blessing doesn't mean you aren't," the woman replied, unfazed. "Whether you meant to or not, our supplies are restored, my children will not go hungry because of you. The favor the Hir has bestowed upon you has brought us relief, and for that I am grateful to you."

When the woman pressed the palm oil firmly back in Ameenah's hands, she did not have the heart to refuse her again. Uneasiness mixed with the guilt in her heart as she watched the woman disappear down the Eastern Road. More came after her, some bearing gifts and blessings, others carrying only words of gratitude and pleas for her to continue to stay in the Hir's graces, for their sake.

When news of the woman behind the Hir's decrees reached the chiefs of local villages and nearby provinces, they saw another use for Ameenah: as a pawn to gain influence over the Hir.

"What girl would not want to have the attention of the Hir," asked Chief Benazi, a burly middle-aged man from the southern village of Derk Miseso where the favor of the Hir had only recently descended.

"You could become the Hir's Ja Heri," he added, looking at her with gleaming, watery eyes. "What woman would not want this?" There was an edge of accusation in his stern voice.

"I can think of nothing I would want less, Sa Min Benazi," Ameenah retorted.

"Then perhaps you should think less of your own wants and more of those of your people," he snapped. The crowd around them murmured in agreement as they watched the exchange.

"Just as you have put my needs above your own?" Ameenah replied.

Only then did he break his gaze.

"No, Sa Min. I will make my own way, just as you make yours."

"We shall see!" Chief Benazi huffed before storming away.

The crowd left quickly after Chief Benazi's departure, some looking back with sympathy, others with fear.

That night, over the simple dinner she prepared for herself and Opa of injera and yellow daal, Ameenah's cheeks burned red with worry and doubt.

"It's as if they believe I hold their lives in my hands," she confided while handing Opa a steaming plate of food.

"In some ways, you do."

Opa Maru, from the province of Harat, had never been coy with his words, but sometimes his honesty still shocked Ameenah as it had the first day they met. She had hired him along with a small crew to help with her first harvest. After half a day of pulling and digging, she had more crops than she had planned for and no idea how to manage the production with the tools she had.

Opa told her plainly that while he admired her talent for cultivation, it was clear she had no idea how to run a farm. It could have cost him his job, but instead of taking her money knowing that half her crops would go to waste, he offered his help. Despite her embarrassment, Ameenah took his advice gratefully. Through the years, Opa's unflinching honesty and earnest friendship made him one of the few people Ameenah knew she could trust.

"Do you think? Do you think I should encourage him?" What he might say next terrified her, but she had to know.

Opa put down the dollop of injera mixed with yellow daal in his hands and looked up into the clear night sky.

"For once, it would be nice to think that one person can solve all the world's problems, to believe that you might be that person, the *only* person, who can make a difference, even if you choose not to."

Ameenah's heart sank as she listened to his words, steeling herself for what she must do.

"But I have lived to see many suns, Ameenah, and I know that life is never that simple. There is never just one road, just one way, just one person. That is not how problems start; it is never how they end."

"Then what are you saying?"

"I have never seen you doubt yourself so. It is easy enough to hear your own voice when you are alone, Ameenah, but holding firm in a crowd of shouting is something you have yet to learn. But no matter how you feel inside, the truth is, you already know what you must do."

Ameenah closed her eyes. If she let go of the looks in the villagers' eyes, pleading, demanding and needy... if she ignored the nagging thread of guilt and selfishness that moved like a snake through every thought she had, Ameenah could see the answer as clearly as the stars above.

"I do not belong with him," she whispered finally.

Beside her Opa said nothing. The truth needs no echo.

"But is that enough, Opa? With everything at stake, there must be a better reason for why a match with the Hir will not work."

"How do you think he found you, Ameenah? Do you believe his arrival here was a coincidence?"

Since his visit, Ameenah had given the matter quite a bit of thought.

"No," she replied. "The belt and the Hir's man in Djobi are the only explanation, but why would he come this far for something so small? He hasn't even asked me to make him anything."

"I don't know, but that still doesn't explain *how* he found you." Opa hesitated. "Do you think Kiva would have told someone?"

"No. Kiva would never betray us."

Opa sighed in frustration as the answers they sought eluded him. "There is something more here; something we're not seeing."

"His reason for coming here has nothing to do with love or any change of heart. The Hir is an evil man, and evil men do not change. They may disguise their actions for a time to get what they want, but they do not change."

Beside him, Ameenah shivered as her hand went to the necklace at her throat.

Opa turned to her with a grave look. "I do not know what the Hir wants from you, Ameenah, but whatever it is, we must make sure he does not get it."

CHAPTER 11

The Forbidden Forest

AMEENAH WOKE WITH a start, jolted from her slumber by a dream that would not allow her to rest. In her dream, tendrils of forest mist crept from the roots of the trees, then billowed up waist-deep as it covered the length and width of the farm. Alarmed by its presence, Ameenah called out to Opa, but he was not there. She was alone, and so she ran. The mist followed her up the stairs of her front porch, licking the backs of her calves as she tried to outrun it. Until finally, she slammed the door to the house behind her.

For a moment, Ameenah closed her eyes and believed that she would be safe. But the truth shook the floor beneath her until the walls themselves fell away, leaving her surrounded by dense grey fog. Out of the mist, she saw a tall figure walking towards her on legs that moved unlike any man she'd ever seen. Blood red horns protruded from his narrow head.

"I can't! I can't!" she cried as the creature reached out to her.

"There is no one else," he replied. "There is no one else," he said again as his long fingers tightened around her throat. Ameenah woke up gasping for air, still clawing at the imaginary fingers at her neck.

It made no sense to head to the forest, especially after the dream that awakened her, but Ameenah knew she could not put it off any longer. For weeks, her work around the farm, combined with the steady stream of visitors, had sapped most of her time and energy. But that was not all. She was also terrified to face the creature again. But there was no choice now. Dawn was hours away, and with no hope of going back to sleep, her need to understand the magic behind her mother's necklace finally won out against her fear.

The light of the two moons spanned the circumference of the sky, making her feel more alive than she ever did during the day. *The night is mine*, she thought, as she wrapped herself in her mother's blue shawl and closed the door to her home behind her.

As she crossed from the farm into the forest, her breath rung in her ears, as if the air itself was closing in around her. Light from the moon strained past the thick foliage of the trees to reach the forest floor and illuminate the tiny wibeti flowers that only displayed their iridescent color at night. With no better plan of where she could find the creature she was looking for, Ameenah followed their path.

Clutching the dagger at her side, Ameenah listened to the sound of small animals scurrying through the fallen leaves, insects singing their mating songs, and predators feasting on their evening kill. But though her footsteps were careful, these were not the animals she feared. Given their last encounter, Ameenah did not expect to be welcomed by the creature she sought, but she needed answers: about the wolves, about the Hir and what he might want from her, and, above all else, about her mother.

He won't hurt me, she tried to assure herself. *If he wanted to, he would have done so already.*

Though logic gave her reason enough to move forward, Ameenah found no comfort in it. She knew nothing about this creature and his motives towards her.

But my necklace fascinated him, she remembered. *He called me a true daughter of the Amasiti. That has to be worth something.*

As she followed the path of the shimmering leaves, Ameenah tried to recall what little she knew of the legend of the Amasiti.

No one talked about them anymore except in hushed whispers. Thousands of years ago, it was said that The Great Mother, Amalaki, bequeathed her power over the earth to her female children. To them she gave the power to create life, to bring forth food from the land, and to heal the body. The daughters were said to have traveled to every corner of the world, ensuring Amalaki's gifts of prosperity and wisdom would be shared by all.

But Ameenah had also heard that despite all the good they tried to do, one Amasiti sorcerer—the last sorcerer of Elan—used her power to kill many people, innocent people, in their war against the 1st Hir. As punishment for her crimes, the five provinces agreed under the Elan Accords to banish the Amasiti from Yet in order to prevent them from ever rising again. Though the worship of Amalaki was still observed by the tribes of Harat, other gods and beliefs began to take her place. Until, over time, the worship of Amalaki and the traditions of the Amasiti were forgotten.

A true daughter of Amalaki! How long has it been? the creature had said.

With no answers to the riddles in her mind and no sign of him after walking aimlessly through the forest, Ameenah found the stump of a broken tree and sat down. Despite the chill in the night air, her body felt warm from the walk. Slowly, she loosened the shawl from around her shoulders and pulled out the necklace from inside her tunic.

Can you only see what others tell you to see?

Ameenah stared at the necklace, willing herself to see beyond the crude black stone in her hand, but nothing happened.

A spell, the creature had called it, but who could have done such a thing, Ameenah wondered. *Did my mother have such powers?*

"Yes," a voice called from behind her. "I thought it was you."

Ameenah whirled around, then sprang to her feet. There had been no sound, no warning of his coming.

"I could smell you from clear across the forest. Why do you look so surprised? I assume you are here looking for me, are you not?"

The creature stalked towards her just as he had in her dreams, covered in blood from the tips of the horns protruding from his head to the edge of his razor-sharp nails. His long tongue flicked out of his mouth like a lizard, clearing the blood from his chin and cheeks.

Ameenah stepped away, unable to find her voice.

"You caught me in between meals, I'm afraid. I hope the sight of fresh blood doesn't bother you?" He smiled, displaying bits of blood and flesh between his teeth with obvious pleasure.

What in the world made me think I could do this, Ameenah wondered, too frightened to breathe and too limp with terror to draw her dagger from its sheath. *How could I have willingly walked into this creature's hands?*

The creature in question arched his wide, elegant brows and sighed.

"I find it hard to imagine that you came all this way without a single word to say to me—or have all your many visitors exhaust your tongue? It's been a long time since we've had such a feast laid out before us."

It took a moment for Ameenah to catch the full meaning of his words, but when she finally understood, horror helped her find her voice.

"You wouldn't."

"I already have."

With ragged breaths, she watched as he closed the distance between them, staring down at her with all the satisfaction of a lion with a fresh kill under its paw. Ameenah's mind ran through the various groups of people she had seen over the past month. Her eyes opened wide.

"But... there were children," she stammered.

"Were there?" The creature's long neck craned upwards, pondering the matter. "I don't recall eating any. Mostly spies, I think, sent to keep an eye on you in between the Hir's visits."

Ameenah stared back at him, stunned.

"How could you know that? What... Who are you?"

The creature's eyes were suddenly serious and thoughtful, with no trace of the feral thing he had been only moments ago. In that moment, his face struck her as beautiful and divinely serene, as if he'd stepped out of some pleasant children's fairy tale.

"You are not ready to understand what I am. Why have you come, Ameenah Yemini of the Great Kingdom of Nor, daughter of Fewa?"

She wanted to know who he was, *what* he was, and even more importantly, who he was in relation to her. But there was one thing she wanted to know more than anything else.

"What do you know of my mother?"

His doe-like gaze poured into Ameenah with an intensity that unnerved her, as if he was weighing her very soul with his eyes.

"What do *you* know of your mother?" he replied.

The question took Ameenah by surprise. Her memories of her mother had always existed without need to verify them as truth. Now, in the face of someone who knew more about the necklace around her neck than she did, Ameenah suddenly doubted herself.

"She... She was kind and gentle to my brother and me. People sought her out for her medicines and her garden. She always had the best fruits, the most delicious vegetables."

Ameenah paused, gauging the stability of her own emotions before continuing.

"But she was best known for her weaving. She made beautiful things, no matter what material she used. People would beg her to make things for them, but most of the time she refused. Mostly, she made clothes for my brother, my father, and me."

"What else do you remember?" the creature asked. His voice was deep and soothing as he circled around her. Feeling suddenly relaxed, Ameenah closed her eyes and pictured her mother's face.

"She was beautiful with dark skin and thick wild hair, like mine. She wore bells, so many that every move she made had a sound. Sometimes she wore a belt with bells around her waist and bracelets around her ankles. I think she would take me into the woods and dance with me. I remember my arms stretched wide. I used to try to imitate her movements, but I could never. She was so graceful."

Mist from the roots of the trees crept up from the ground and surrounded her.

As if in a trance made of warm, golden sun, Ameenah's words faded as she lost herself in the memory. Unconsciously, she raised her hands and closed her eyes, dancing with the memory of her mother by the soundless rhythm of the earth beneath her feet.

"Stop!"

The creature shouted so loudly that Ameenah almost lost her footing. Her eyes flew open. The warm feeling drained from her body as she looked around and realized once more where she was and who she was with. The ground was soft and powdery beneath her feet and her cheeks were wet with tears.

"Do you know nothing of the power you wield?"

Ameenah searched for his voice, circling until she found him crouched against the side of a tree with his face turned away from her.

"It's just a dance my mother used to do," she murmured. "I barely remember it."

"And yet, the ground quakes at your beckoning. These things are not meant for others. They are sacred." Slowly, the creature unfolded himself and turned to her in awe.

Ameenah stared back at him, completely dumbfounded. "But you asked. You asked me to remember."

"Have you ever shown that dance to anyone? The Hir?"

"Of course not! I didn't even remember it until this moment."

The creature searched her eyes for lies and found none. His body relaxed as he came close enough for his hand to hover just above her necklace.

"There is no one else. No one else like you." His voice was a reverent whisper. "Your mother was right to keep this power hidden from you."

"My mother. Was she one of the Amasiti?"

The creature stared back at her, silence confirming the truth she now knew.

Ameenah lifted the necklace between them. "Is this what the Hir wants? Is this why he's come for me?"

"Not truly. He cannot see it for what it is. The necklace is only a symbol of a power he craves, but he cannot possess. What he desires can only be given."

"I would never give him anything," Ameenah replied.

"This Hir is much like his fathers before him. He does not seek *anything*. He seeks you."

"I—"

"You cannot be certain what you would or would not do. The Hir is no fool. He will try to lure you to him. He already has, but you must resist no matter the cost."

Ameenah felt a flash of fear at his words, but remained silent.

"This," he continued, tracing the shape of the stone with the tip of a single razor-sharp talon. "is a gift whose purpose has yet to be revealed. It is time for you to leave."

"Go?" Ameenah leaned in ready to reach for the creature before thinking better of it. "But you've hardly told me anything!"

"I didn't need to. You already know more than you realize, more than is safe. The rest you will learn as you must."

"How?" she protested. "I don't even know your name. Who you are?"

"I am of the Sri. That is all you have earned the right to know."

Like the stories, she thought with a shiver.

Seeing the fear his name inspired, the creature smiled at Ameenah, baring his teeth proudly before darting into the trees and galloping away.

CHAPTER 12

The Invitation

RUMORS OF THE Hir's fifth visit had been circulating back and forth for more than two weeks. Though Ameenah loathed his coming, at least this time she was prepared.

On the day he finally arrived, the ground shook beneath her feet as he approached. All morning Ameenah had been pulling weeds from the ground, turning the dirt from the garden with her bare hands to distract her from the dull dread of his presence.

When he arrived, she rose to greet him exactly as she intended, hands and dress filthy and a face smeared with grime. Ameenah paused as the largest entourage she'd ever seen poured from the Eastern Road, almost eclipsing her view of the forest behind them. As he always did, the Hir stopped directly in front of her gate while his fearsome guard stood at attention a few feet behind him.

"Ja Hir," she said quietly. "You honor me with your presence, unexpected though it is."

"I see," he replied, taking in her disheveled state. "Perhaps I should have sent someone ahead to announce my arrival."

"Forgive my current state, Ja Hir. I pray my appearance does not offend you." Ameenah dipped her head when she could no longer contain her smirk. Behind her, Opa kicked at her heel.

"It is a testament to your beauty that it has not," the Hir admitted as he dismounted his horse.

Disappointed by the fact that her appearance had not been able to drive him away as planned, Ameenah met his gaze, determined to end his visit as soon as possible.

"How may I be of service, Ja Hir?"

"As you are no doubt aware, the 400th anniversary of the Elan Peace Accords is in a month's time. To commemorate the occasion and reestablish peaceful ties between the five provinces, I have chosen to host a grand celebration in its honor. It is time we reinforce our commitment to the alliance that binds our lands together. I have traveled all this way to invite you to accompany me as my personal guest. With you by my side, I know we can silence the discord between the provinces and unify our people once more."

Ameenah was speechless.

Of all the scenarios she had imagined, Ameenah had *never* considered this. His words made no sense to her. Of course, she had heard about the anniversary and impending celebration, and she had every intention of ignoring it as she had done every other year. How could she, a farmer from The Forbidden Forest, have any role whatsoever in the unification of Yet? The City of Mera Meja, where the ball would be held, was the capital of Yet and the very heart of elite society—everything Ameenah had spent her life trying to avoid. To be ushered into that world on his arm? Ameenah could not imagine a worse fate.

Opa's second kick to Ameenah's heel brought her back to her senses and the realization that she had not uttered a single word since the Hir extended his invitation. Ameenah took in the scene in front of her anew. The Hir's soldiers surrounded them on three sides. What she had first mistaken as an entourage she now understood for its true intent—an army meant to threaten her and those she cared for if she dared refuse him.

Silently, Ameenah counted the people at her farm—Opa and two workers he'd just hired from the bushlands of Harat. They were few, yet still too many. Regardless of her own personal battles, she had no right to risk their lives. Desperation gave way to relief as Opa stepped close beside her. Despite the danger that surrounded them, his back was straight and his eyes were focused ahead. His message to her was clear: He would not be cowed and neither should she. Ameenah returned her attention to the Hir, resolved in what she must do.

Impatient with her silence, the Hir addressed her with a voice that was sharp with aggravation.

"Have you nothing to say to your Hir?" he said, stepping towards her, but Ameenah had inherited her father's height. Her eyes were almost level with his.

Pleased to see the veneer of calm slip from his demeanor, Ameenah smiled up at him and answered.

"You extend a great honor to me, Ja Hir, but I must decline. I am not fit to stand beside a man such as yourself."

She hoped her words sounded sweet, for she meant them to settle in and sting like poison.

The Hir covered his anger in a mask of amused sympathy.

"The invitation of the Hir is not easily given," he cautioned.

"Yes, an honor that is wasted on a simple woman. There are many others who would—"

"There are no others," he snapped. "No other like you, Ameenah. Believe me when I tell you I have searched the world for one such as you." His hand trembled as it reached out for her, then stilled. "There is no one else, my dear."

She did not know why, but the force of his words made her shiver with dread. Ameenah's mouth went dry as she scoured her brain for a reason that would allow her to refuse him while still saving the lives of those around her.

I must find a way out of this, she thought. Nervously she wiped the mud from her hands on to the front of her dress. Abruptly, the Hir stepped back from the plume of dried dust that crumbled to the ground, lest it land upon his fine boots.

Ameenah almost laughed before a new idea occurred to her.

"Ja Hir," she said softly, meeting his eyes once more. "Though you have chosen to see past the dirt and grime that make up my simple life, others may not be as sympathetic as you are. Where should a farmer like myself acquire the finery required to stand at your side as all the governors and nobility of our land look to you for guidance?"

The Hir's eyes narrowed over her again as if reacquainting himself with a foul stench. Sensing her chance, Ameenah continued.

"Nothing should distract from the vision of greatness you would seek to impart. It pains me to say that even my best clothes are not fit for such an occasion, Ja Hir."

The Hir took another step back, appraising her with fresh disdain. With delight she felt him finally taking in the hard work she had put in to make herself truly unacceptable in his eyes.

"You are wise, young Ameenah, to have brought this to my attention," he began as he made a slow circle around her. "It is true that I could not bring you to the palace in such a state."

Ameenah held her breath in anticipation, waiting for him to declare his recent overtures a grave mistake.

"I will have a gown made for you. One fitting of your place beside me." The Hir smiled broadly despite her devastated expression. Speechless once more, Ameenah could only watch, as the Hir mounted his horse.

"The celebration will begin in a month. Your dress will be ready before then. I will send one of my guardsmen to deliver it to you personally."

Before Ameenah could offer another word of protest, the Hir turned his horse and rode away, with an army of followers behind him.

CHAPTER 13

The Message & The Messenger

THE HIR'S VISIT shook Ameenah to her core. She had spent every day following his departure trying desperately to find a way to resist his advances without putting Opa and the farm in danger. For three days, she worried continuously as she went about her work without coming up with a single viable solution. On the fourth day the province governors sent their best representative, who descended on her home without warning.

When she first saw Rahmeel coming down the Eastern Road, Ameenah barely recognized him. Gone were the flowing, elegant robes she'd seen him wear in Djobi. Instead, he traveled alone in simple riding clothes with a knapsack on his back.

"When Kiva told me where you lived, I didn't believe it," Rahmeel called as he pulled his horse up to the front gate and dismounted. His eyes surveyed the length of the farm in awe.

"But seeing it for myself, I must admit there is a strange beauty in this madness." His voice rumbled with laughter.

"Rahmeel?" she asked in disbelief. "What are you doing here?" Ameenah wiped her hands on her apron while searching the distance behind him. "Did Nasir send you?"

"No. According to the last message I received from him, Nasir is still up north. He's not due back for several weeks." The crestfallen expression on Ameenah's face made Rahmeel laugh. "I may not be my brother, but I hope I'm still welcome in my sister's house." His smile was broad and genuine.

"Of course you are," she smiled. "I'm just surprised to see *you* so far from the cities."

As he closed the distance between them, their embrace was warm but brief.

"Indeed. The only place close to here is forbidden," he replied. His eyes shifted to the strange mist that hovered in the trees. The Forbidden Forest loomed too close for his liking.

"Yes," she replied with a knowing gaze. "What has driven you so far from the comforts of home?"

"I wanted to see you," he said as he stood back to look at her. Though the dirt on her apron made it obvious that she had been working in the field all day, Rahmeel marveled at how lovely she was.

Like her mother, he thought, though his memory of Fewa was not sharp enough to be certain.

"And I need to talk with you."

Ameenah wasn't sure if it was the sense of apprehension in his voice or the firm set of his jaw, but suddenly she knew exactly why he had come. Abruptly, she turned, heading back to her garden with Rahmeel following closely behind.

"I already told everyone who would listen, I am not going to the celebration with the Hir. So if that's why you came all this way, you've wasted your time."

"Ameenah!" The sharpness in his tone made her halt her steps.

"This is serious!" Rahmeel stepped in front to block her path. "There are larger things at stake here."

"Is that so?" Her eyes on him were angry, defiant.

Rahmeel took a deep breath before continuing.

"Yes, Ameenah. Things have gotten much worse since you left, much more complicated than you know."

"I left all those *complications* and moved here," she replied, pointing a dirty index finger towards the earth. "so I wouldn't have to know. I don't want any part of this."

"But you *are* a daughter of Yet from a noble house. No amount of dirt can cover that up. Yet needs you, Ameenah. Whether you like it or not, we are all dependent upon each other. There's more at stake than your comfort or even mine. Something is coming, and if we don't stand together against this threat, none of us will be safe. Your way of life will not survive."

"What do you mean?"

"There are many things we need to discuss. More than I could tell you myself. That is why I have come first, to urge you to listen. The others will be here by morning."

Rahmeel was true to his word. By the next morning, before the first sun had begun to appear in the western sky, the Governors of Anam and Mir had already arrived.

If they had come to her as strangers, it would have been easy enough to throw them off her land. Ameenah was the sole land-keeper of her parcel, the only one with the right to reap the fruits of her labor and keep it as her own. As such, no one could claim the right to be on her land without her permission, as long as she maintained it.

But they did not come as strangers. They'd sent Rahmeel a day ahead of their delegation to ensure they would not be turned away. And because she and Rahmeel had known each other as children, Ameenah allowed them into her home.

With barely any time to prepare and no room to host them all within the confines of her modest home, they gathered outside under a tent the governors' servants erected. The morning air carried an unusual chill, forcing the three governors from the provinces of Anam, Mir, and Nor to huddle close together over her breakfast fire, looking anxious and wary as their gazes drifted from the border of the Forbidden Forest to the Eastern Road. As she and Opa served them the morning meal, she wondered whether it was the foreboding nature of their surroundings, the air of secrecy around their gathering, or the weight of their own schemes that made them all seem so unsettled. Ameenah knew these men were accustomed to more lavish accommodations, but the scarcity of comforts gave her hope that their visit would be brief. Once she had served the last of the coffee to the gathering elders, Rahmeel began.

"Ameenah, we thank you for your hospitality and for accommo-dating us, despite the short notice you were given. Under normal circumstances, we would have sent word of our impending arrival, but…" He hesitated. "In truth, we were afraid that you would refuse, and we could not take that risk."

Ameenah's jaw tightened. Despite the fact that she hated being cornered, she decided not to protest. Arguing would only prolong whatever it was they came to say, and that was not her goal. Instead, she took a breath to calm herself and studied the faces of the men around her. Ameenah didn't think she recognized anyone until her eyes settled on a man who stood tall despite the many years he carried. In his face, she saw the memories of her past. Raw emotion gripped her as the man turned to her and spoke.

"It has been a long time since you played with Nasir, Rahmeel, and Kiva in my courtyard, Ameenah. Do you remember who I am?" he asked gently.

Ameenah shook her head, trying to keep the memories from rushing forth. When the lump in her throat stopped her from answering, he continued.

"I am Jaleen Ebibi, the Governor of Nor and father to Rahmeel, Nasir, and Kiva. You may not recognize me now, but I have known you since you were a child. I knew your parents and your beloved brother. I know, more than most, the forces that have driven you to this dreadful place at the end of all that is safe. Nasir and Kiva have told me of your life here. We have not come to disturb what little peace you've found. We have come because we have no other choice."

"Though it may not appear so to you, Yet is on the brink of war. In every province, we have been attacked by bandits and thieves. Crime unlike anything any of us have experienced before plagues our towns, threatening our families and children. Some would have us believe that this is the work of raiders from Ashat and Harat, but our investigations do not prove this to be true."

Ameenah watched a ripple of shock move through the group, as if Jaleen's announcement was as unknown to everyone else as it was to her. As fear passed across each face, Ameenah knew it was not a farce.

Umar Ofessa, the governor of Anam, was a short, unassuming man, but when he spoke, his voice boomed across the tent. "What investigation? You have proof of this treachery you claim?"

"I do," Jaleen replied cautiously. "But I did not dare speak of it until I could see you all face-to-face. Only those who would risk coming here in person can be trusted."

Immediately, Ameenah noticed that the sigils from two provinces were missing, Harat and Kiveer.

"I would caution, Sa Min, against reading too much into the absence of our colleagues," Saveer Etefu, the youthful governor of Mir, replied. "Harat has been at war with all of us in one way or another for 400 years. They hate everything and everyone outside their borders." Ameenah watched Opa stiffen at Saveer's comments towards his homeland, but he remained silent as the governor continued.

"And I can only imagine how closely the governor of Kiveer is being watched. Making the trip to the edge of the Forbidden Forest is a fool's errand by any measure. Let us say our piece and be done. We linger here at great risk to ourselves and those we seek to protect."

Ignoring the impatient expression on Saveer's face, Jaleen continued. "Practical as ever, Sa Min Saveer, but trust is a risk, one that requires sacrifice to earn."

"As many of you know, a small portion of our guard has been in pursuit of these bandits for some time. Our armies have crossed your borders to drive these criminals from our lands as is our duty to each of you as sworn allies. However, we've also commissioned a separate group of men, who have been tracking the marauders in secret to determine from whence they have come. We have over a dozen groups employed in this pursuit. So far, what we've found is that while the bandits appear to come from different customs and speak different languages; none we have tracked ever move out of the borders of Yet. In fact, their movements center around two main locations: the Poison Mountain and the catacombs just south of the capitol in Kiveer. We believe these are their bases of operation, although we cannot confirm their purpose."

While the governors looked to each other with growing concern, Jaleen fixed his gaze on Ameenah.

"We believe the Hir is behind these bandits, using them to destabilize our provinces so that when he strikes, our people will be too weak to respond, but we won't know for sure until we can place someone in his inner circle."

Ameenah's eyes widened as their intentions for her became clear. "And you want me to somehow be this person?"

"Yes," Jaleen replied. "The Hir's interest in you gives us the best opportunity we've had to gain more intimate access to him and his plans."

"And what makes you think that he would let me close enough to know any of his secrets?"

"Because he is infatuated with you," Jaleen replied. "Despite your many rebuffs, he has chosen to pursue you. I believe we can use his interest to our advantage to protect the people of Yet."

Sa Min Umar spoke next.

"The Hir rarely ventures from his palace, much less Mera Meja. Yet, he has done so for you, many times as we understand it. None of us have been invited into his private chambers, but if you could get into his office and listen in on his private Council meetings, the information would be invaluable to us."

Ameenah could hardly believe what she was hearing. By her assessment, the Hir was at best toying with her in hopes of getting her mother's necklace from her. Once he realized she would not give in, his interest would surely turn hostile, if not lethal. Unfortunately, it was clear that the men before her expected her to take the thread of the Hir's interest and weave it into something more. She shuddered with repulsion at the thought.

"And how far do you expect me to take this infatuation?"

"As far as you need to in order to gain his trust," Jaleen replied.

The words hit her as if they were a blow to the face. "So you expect me to sell myself to this man who you believe is evil. A man you say wants to kill us all!"

"No, Ameenah," Jaleen replied, calmly. "We want you to use his attention to help us defeat him, to keep our country from war."

"Many women would consider it a great honor to claim the affection of the Hir," Sa Min Umar added. "Even if you were only his concubine, we have no reason to believe that he would mistreat you. It is a small price to pay for your country, and it would surely be a better life then you could ever hope to achieve on your own in this horrid place."

Ameenah leapt to her feet. "Then throw one of your own daughters at his feet! You think that because I am alone, my life is so worthless that I would allow you to come here and sell me for your cause?"

"Calm yourself, Ameenah. That is not what was said," Jaleen replied.

"But it *is* what was meant!"

"It is not our desire to force you," Rahmeel offered, but the flash of rage that burned in Ameenah's eyes told him that he'd chosen his words poorly.

"As if you could," she spat.

Seeing Ameenah's fingers grip the hilt of her dagger, Rahmeel put his hands up in a gesture of open surrender.

"I didn't mean to imply—" Rahmeel began, but his plea was overcome by the rumbling voice of the governor of Anan.

"This is absurd!" he declared, pounding his large wooden staff into the earth. "Is there no father or uncle alive to bring this girl to heel, Jaleen?"

Ameenah shook with rage as the hot, unfamiliar feeling of being publicly ridiculed scorched her cheeks. She scanned the gathering of barely-familiar faces. Just like the night the bandits attacked her home, once again she was outnumbered. She'd heard stories of girls being dragged off in the night against their will to be married. Never had she imagined that she could ever become one of them. Besides Rahmeel and Opa, there was no one she truly knew, and even fewer she could trust.

Of the two men, Ameenah knew that Opa would lay down his life for her without question, which was not at all what she wanted. On the other hand, Rahmeel could be counted on to be decent as long as he could preserve his own agenda, but in this case, Ameenah was not sure whose allegiance he would choose if he was forced to do so. There were eleven men in all, and though Ameenah was surrounded, she had never felt so alone in her life.

Jaleen let out an exasperated sigh. "We need her as an *ally*," he snapped, giving Umar a chastening glare. "How would this work if..."

"If what, Father?"

The entire party turned as Nasir and his men emerged from the trees behind them, as silent as a whisper. Ameenah tried her best to keep the tears from falling down her cheeks as Nasir came to stand beside her. His clothing was different, ragged and rough-ly-hewn compared to the uniform he usually wore, but Ameenah could not recall ever being happier to see him and the retinue of warriors at his back.

"If she is forced to be used and corrupted by a man so evil he would hire mercenaries to slaughter his own people?"

The governor of Mir frowned, disturbed by the venom in Nasir's voice . "You speak as if he were an animal."

"He is worse than that," Nasir replied. "Animals kill only for survival."

"And you have proof of this?" Saveer pressed. His gaze flick-ered from Nasir to his father.

"We do," Nasir replied, avoiding his father's cautious gaze. "I've received reports from our team of spies in the north. They've been tracking a band of raiders they believe are responsible for destroy-ing dozens of villages across the northeast. Our men tracked them along the western border of Mir to the Poison Mountain. We received confirmation that the bandits entered a passage guarded by members of the Hir's own private forces. Our team sent a few men in to follow them, but none returned."

A rumble of shock thundered through the gathering.

"And how do you know these spies of yours can be trusted?" Umar demanded. "They could easily be agents of some foreign usurper sent here to stir up trouble."

Jaleen met the governor's eyes squarely. "These are no usurper's pawns, Umar. Their messages are sent directly to Rahmeel who would certainly know the difference."

"The threat is real, Sa Min Saveer," Nasir added. "I would not tell you if it were not so."

Umar Ufessa leaned back in his chair, folding his robes around him like a shield.

"Why the Poison Mountain?" Saveer wondered aloud.

"We do not yet know," Nasir admitted. "There were too few men left in their camp to risk further losses. As soon as I received their report, I came here to gain authorization to gather more men and return to the site in force."

"That would be unwise," Sa Min Umar warned. "The Poison Mountain has been abandoned for centuries. I regret the loss of your men, but why should we move our armies to the outermost reaches of Yet when our people are in danger right here? No. It is more imperative that we move forward with our plan to gain as much leverage as we can over the Hir." Umar's eyes returned to Ameenah once more.

"There must be another way," Nasir said, straining to keep his gaze from the woman at his side.

"Much has happened since you've been away," his father replied gently. "The Hir has shown great favor towards Ameenah and every village that surrounds her. He has offered protection and resources to recover from the scourge of the raids. Not a single raid has occurred since his first visit to her."

"That only proves my point," Nasir replied.

"That is why we must press our advantage," Umar urged.

"Ameenah is not a pawn for you to play!" Nasir's voice was low but furious.

"Brother," Rahmeel interjected. "Calm yourself. You're hardly objective in this matter."

Nasir's nostrils flared as he stared down his brother in silence.

"My interests do not matter here. None of ours do. Only Ameenah can decide."

"All right then," Saveer said. "You know what is at stake. Tell us, Sha El Ameenah, what is your decision?"

The presence of Nasir and his Simbu-Ki had given Ameenah a moment to regain her composure. Beside her, Nasir's eyes burned like searing coals pressed against her cheek, but she could not meet his gaze.

Though his presence lessened the immediate threat of simply being snatched away by the governors, the danger around her felt so close she could barely summon enough air in her lungs to speak. Though she was far from indifferent to the suffering of her people, Ameenah knew she could never do what they asked of her. Her eyes settled on Jaleen as she prepared to send them all away, but as she opened her mouth to speak, one of Nasir's soldiers burst from the hidden path behind the trees.

"Nasir! The Hir is coming! He is almost upon us!"

Nasir turned to Ameenah. "Hide!"

The governor of Anam was the first to stand, but Jaleen raised his hand to keep him where he was.

"Stay," he commanded them all. "We should not be found with armed guards among us, but the rest of us must stay."

Though he hated the idea of leaving Ameenah's side, Nasir knew his father was right. With a wave of his hands, he ordered his men back to their hiding places, but he could not go himself. He held Ameenah's gaze, then motioned towards the back fence, making sure she understood that he would not be far away.

Nasir barely had time to tuck himself away before the Hir's royal carriage appeared. Ameenah stepped forward, anxious to draw any attention away from Nasir as the Hir's carriage stopped. The governors made an uneasy line behind her as the carriage door flew open. A tall, spindly man emerged, looking over the gathering with suspicion in his eyes. Ameenah recognized him immediately.

"Governors," Jogg sneered. "The Hir will be most interested to know I found you all gathered here."

Jaleen stepped beside Ameenah. "Yes, Sa Min Jogg. It is a pleasant surprise that we meet. I believe we are here on common purpose."

"How so?"

"I assume we are both here to encourage our countrywoman to accept the generous invitation of the Hir to join us in the celebration of the Peace Accords."

Jogg was skeptical, but no less taken aback by Jaleen's open greeting.

"The Hir's desire is his subject's command," Jogg replied coolly before finally acknowledging Ameenah.

"Ameenah of the Forbidden Forest," he said with a nod.

The young woman before him looked familiar, but less somehow than what she had been in the tavern in Djobi.

There she had been wrapped in fine silks, a woman who could at least be trained to be worthy of the Hir, he thought. But taking in her appearance now, with her dusty clothes and the wild trappings of the forest, he was less sure of who she might be.

"I am," she replied, tickled by the title he'd given her despite the accusation in it.

"Then this is for you." Without ceremony, he placed a parcel wrapped in delicate blood-red linen in her hands. Despite the considerable size of the package, it folded easily within her grasp.

"A gift from the Hir."

"I can't," Ameenah began, immediately extending her arms to give it back. The weight of the package struck her as unexpectedly heavy and as she glanced down to discover why, she became immediately transfixed by the hint of shimmer she could just make out under the gauzy linen.

"He will accept no refusal, girl!" Jogg said, recoiling from her. "What you hold there was woven by the finest seamstress in the palace and I will not carry it back only to lose my head over the likes of *you*! Enough blood has been spilled on your account. I have done what he bid me. See that you heed the lords of this land and make your way to the feast. No one else should suffer for your folly."

He turned then without another word, slammed the carriage door shut and rode away.

But Ameenah barely heard a word of what he said as she held the package in her arms.

Behind her, the governor of Mir let out a loud sigh. "This was a mistake," Sa Min Saveer declared. "We must leave now before the Hir's emissary brings word of our gathering to his ears."

Rahmeel shrugged. "With any luck, Jogg will think we are on the Hir's side."

"Are you *mad*?!" the governor of Anam bellowed. "He already suspects us!"

While the governors argued amongst themselves, their servants rushed to pack their masters' things and travel home with haste.

But amidst the commotion, Nasir watched Ameenah who was silent and focused on the parcel in her hand despite the confusion that surrounded her.

CHAPTER 14

Calling

IGNORED AND UNNOTICED by all but one, Ameenah turned, cradling the package in her arms as she walked up the steps to her home. Once inside, she placed the parcel on her kitchen table and unwrapped the delicate fabric, revealing a dress made of pale gold fabric.

Her fingers trembled in awe as she pulled the gown from the red linen and held it up to the light coming through her window. The dress hung like armor yet felt like silk. Behind her, Nasir gasped.

Though the cut of the dress was simple, a sleeveless gown with a tapered waist and flowing skirt, the material and craftsmanship were exquisite. In the noonday sun, the dress shone as if it were alive with fire, a blazing shield of molten gold against the light. Yet it was as supple to the touch as her own leather. There could only be one creator of a garment such as this, and Ameenah knew now that she would attend any celebration with anyone for the chance to meet her.

"Ameenah, what is it?"

How can I put this feeling into words?

"I don't know," Ameenah whispered. "It's like I know this dress somehow." Her hands caressed the fabric. It felt like tiny, flat seashells against her palm.

"Have you seen it before?"

"No. Never, but that's not what I mean. I can't explain it, but it's like the dress reminds me of something… or someone."

Tears sprang to her eyes. *It can't be,* she told herself. *It can't be.*

Nasir drew near enough to hear the unevenness of her breathing. "Who does it remind you of?"

It took a moment before Ameenah could say the words out loud.

"My mother," she whispered. "She would have worn a dress like this, beautiful and fierce, like a warrior."

The garment was stunning, Nasir couldn't deny it. But as he watched the dress transfix her, he couldn't help but wonder if there wasn't something else at play.

"Ameenah, tell me truly. Do you want to go to the celebration with him?"

Though his words felt far away, they still had the power to break the spell she was under. Ameenah folded the dress in half and placed it on the table without looking at him.

"Is that a serious question?"

"It's an honest one," Nasir replied, studying the frown on her face. "I know you hate him, but there is more at stake than just your feelings. Maybe you've decided that my father and the other governors are right. That the benefit to Yet outweighs whatever personal cost there may be."

Ameenah turned and met his gaze. "Is that what you think? That Yet would be better off if I were with him."

Shame and jealousy made him turn from her gaze.

"No," he said finally. "But what I think, what I want, doesn't matter."

Slowly, she raised one hand to touch his cheek. His beard was a thick, rich black, silky to the touch despite how worn and rough he looked. His eyes met hers again, weary and vulnerable.

"It matters to me." Her voice was gentle with all the steel he needed to hear behind it. "The governors, the people in the towns and villages that visit my home almost every day, all of them ask me to appease the Hir, to think of Yet, but none of them see the truth. He is using us, *all* of us. You know it. I know it and I have no intention of making myself a pawn in whatever game this is."

Ameenah waited until she saw the tension ease from Nasir's eyes before she continued.

"This has nothing to do with the Hir or the Accord celebrations," she added. "I don't want to go, but I need to understand why this dress pulls my memories so strongly. I need to know why it reminds me of her. I don't ever remember my mother wearing a dress like this, but if it was hers, I need to know. Maybe it will help me understand something about what happened to her after she was taken."

Nasir's eyes roamed over the dress once more. "It doesn't look old to me," he admitted.

"No, it doesn't," she agreed, relieved that he'd noticed the same thing she did. "What if she's alive, Nasir?! What if she's somewhere locked away in the palace in Mera Meja? If there's even the smallest chance that she's alive, that I could find her, I have to take it."

Ameenah's eyes gleamed as she looked up at Nasir, searching for a spark of hope that he could not give. She wanted him to believe, to cling with her to the fragile notion that they could find her mother alive, but the idea filled Nasir with dread. If the Hir held her mother alive and had done so for the past seventeen years, he could only imagine the horrors she must have endured at his hands—horrors that Nasir hoped Ameenah would never know.

"Meena," he began cautiously.

"I know," she said, closing her eyes against the tears. "It could just be a coincidence, but… I *know* it's not, Nasir. I *feel* it."

"Okay," he said, bringing her into his embrace. "Okay."

Her voice was muffled as she pressed into him. "I need to know, Nasir."

"I understand," he replied, holding her tightly as he wracked his brain for a way to verify who the dress belonged to or how it was made. "I will help you find the answers you need."

For a long while they stood in her kitchen. Nasir stroked Ameenah's hair in silence, letting his fingers slip through her mass of curls. Suddenly an idea came to him. "Perhaps, we should take the dress to…"

"Siama," they said together. Ameenah looked up at him and smiled.

"Yes," he agreed. "Siama will know what to do."

An hour later, they began their trip on the Eastern Road, each lost in their own thoughts yet grateful for the rare occasion to enjoy each other's company. Nasir pondered how much had changed since the last time he'd seen Ameenah and if she truly understood how unlikely it was that she would ever be able to return to the sheltered life she'd had before.

At least now she knows the threat from the Hir is real.

His thoughts ran to the Poison Mountain and the strange chanting he'd heard there. The memory sent an icy shiver down his spine. Silently, he tried to guess how much time they had before the secret of whatever the Hir was truly up to was unleashed. *Not long*, he feared. *Not long.*

Beside him, Ameenah marveled at the irony of having pushed Nasir away the last time they'd met, only to be traveling alone with him now. When he'd showed up at her farm during the meeting with the governors, she'd never been more relieved for his friendship, his presence, and his love.

A love I have yet to admit to him.

Slowly, she pulled Ifa back, allowing her some space to look at Nasir without being noticed. Though she was sure he knew she shared his feelings, at some point, she would have to gather up the courage to say the words—out loud.

I owe him that much, though he would never ask me to repay the debt.

Trailing behind by several paces, Ameenah admired the expanse of muscles that flexed beneath his fitted cotton tunic. A frown crossed her face as she took in the coarse design, with haphazard seams that went across the back and arms of the garment. It looked like the shirt had been made from scraps of different fabric and repaired several times in its well-worn life. Nasir's trousers were no better.

Where is his uniform? Ameenah wondered. She knew Nasir was not a man who was overly concerned with his appearance, but his clothes, though simple, were always beautifully made. He had not looked like this when she'd last seen him.

His clothes must have something to do with his mission in the north, Ameenah guessed. From his profile, Ameenah could tell that Nasir was deep in thought. *Mulling over his secrets*, she suspected. When her curiosity became too powerful to ignore, Ameenah closed the distance between them.

"So tell me where you've been."

At first, Nasir was quiet as they rode down the secret path to Siama's house. "I told you I was headed north," he said finally, avoiding her gaze.

Ameenah waited for him to continue, but Nasir's silence stretched on until she grew suspicious. Looking at him, Ameenah smirked as she watched Nasir look in every direction but hers.

He's hiding something, she thought, before remembering his father's words from the governors' meeting. Ameenah moved Ifa closer to Nasir's horse, Tewa, then began wondering aloud.

"All right, Tewa, why don't *you* tell me," she said with a wink at the beautiful brown horse at her side. The horse drifted closer, lifting his large head and braying loudly as if to answer her question. When Nasir chuckled, but refused to take the bait, she continued.

"Your father mentioned that he'd been working with a group of spies to find out who the bandits are working for. He made it sound like they were part of some outside group, but now I'm wondering if you weren't a part of it. Is that why you're dressed so strangely?"

Nasir's eyes flashed toward her, then shook his head in amusement.

"When did he say all that? And since when are you so nosy," he teased.

"I am not," she protested as Nasir's laughter grew.

"I just had a group of old men descend upon my home and try to sell me off to the Hir so that I could be *their* spy. I think I deserve some answers!"

Nasir slowed Tewa to a stop across the road, blocking their path forward.

"You do," he said earnestly, meeting her gaze. "I'm sorry they said those things. I didn't hear it all, but I heard enough."

"They think that just because I'm a woman and young, they know what's best for me better than I do," Ameenah scowled. "And don't apologize for them. You're nothing like that."

"They're only foolish enough to think those things because they don't know you," Nasir replied.

Ameenah's lips curled with the faintest smile.

"But I am sorry," he continued. "I know my father has been desperate to find a way into the Hir's inner circle, but I never thought he would go this far."

"I told you, none of this is your doing. You have nothing to apologize for."

Nasir searched her eyes, making sure there was no trace of the frightened woman whom he had found standing in the middle of the gathering of governors. Though she hid it from them, Nasir knew her well enough to see the fear behind the fury in her eyes. Pleased to see the Ameenah he knew fully restored, Nasir directed Tewa back, allowing Ameenah to lead their way forward.

"But is it as bad as your father says?"

"It may be worse, from what I have been able to gather on our missions," Nasir replied. Ameenah nodded slowly, acknowledging the secret he was sharing with her. "From what we can tell, the bandits are organized and trained at some compound just outside of Yet, but most of them are from our lands, and their allegiances all point back to Mera Meja. We tracked the bandits delivering bounties and men to the Poison Mountain, then watched gold from the mountain being brought to the capital, guarded and watched by the same bandits."

"And you're certain this all goes back to the Hir?"

"Yes. My father and the governors still think that there is a diplomatic way to solve this through blackmail or some sort of political alliance. That's why the Hir's sudden attention towards you is of such interest to them, but my instincts tell me that it is far too late for that."

"Why do you think so?" Ameenah asked, watching the worry on his face.

"Because of the Mountain," Nasir replied. "I can't explain it, Ameenah, but something evil lurks within that place. The Hir would not go to such lengths to keep his schemes a secret if the reward were not great. His attempts at diplomacy are a ruse."

"For what purpose?" she asked.

Nasir's frown deepened as he sighed. "To keep us distracted while he amasses a power greater than anything we have the means to resist."

They arrived to find Siama hanging laundry in her backyard. As always, she didn't seem truly surprised to see them.

"Now this is a pretty sight," she sang as she greeted them, taking Ameenah and then Nasir into her warm embrace.

"To what do I owe the honor of *both* your company?" Siama asked playfully.

"We need your help," Ameenah replied. "The Hir has asked me to accompany him to the Accords Celebration."

"What? How can that be?" The alarm in Siama's voice twisted the knot in Nasir's stomach.

"The Hir's been visiting her with some regularity. Ameenah seems to have captured his attention," he added.

"When?" Siama asked. With no need to travel to the city, it had been months since she was privy to the latest gossip. "How did he find out where she lived?"

"I've been wondering that same thing myself," Nasir muttered.

"He and his men came to my farm, a week after I returned home from Djobi. They said they were surveying the damage caused by the raids when his men stumbled upon my farm, but I can't help but think that the belt I told you about in Djobi somehow led them to me," Ameenah explained.

Siama's eyes narrowed in disbelief.

"Why would he leave his palace in Mera Meja to inspect a raid?" Nasir asked before Siama could pose the same question.

"He would not," Siama said. "Not without another purpose."

"It doesn't matter," Ameenah continued. "I told him I would not go. But he had something made for me anyway. Something I need you to see."

Though Ameenah's voice was calm, Siama felt a growing sense of uneasiness as she watched the young woman open the satchel at her hip and pull out a package wrapped in red linen.

Siama felt its power the moment she saw it, rippling through the air like an ancient whisper from long ago. Before Ameenah could begin unwrapping the first layer, Siama spoke up.

"Not here! Come inside, both of you."

Siama herded Ameenah and Nasir inside and locked the door behind them. After taking a moment to gather herself by the front door, she turned to find the contents of the package Ameenah had brought laid out on the small table at the center of her home. Siama stood for a long time, transfixed by the way the surface of the garment fractured the candlelight in the room. Golden sparks flew across the walls, alive with their own light and fire.

How long has it been since I've seen the power of a true Amasiti, she thought. Her body trembled with anticipation. Yet in all her long years, she had never witnessed anything quite like this—magic that was older than the ground underneath her feet. Siama felt the current rise up like ancient legends from the ash coming back to reclaim what was lost and make it new.

"Is it my mother's?" Ameenah asked. Her voice trembled with hope.

"Of course it is, child. There is no other with the power to create such magic. Can you not hear her voice?"

Tears welled in Ameenah's eyes. "It calls to me. I feel it in my flesh."

Nasir stepped closer, taking Ameenah under his arm.

"How is this possible?" he asked. "I thought Fewa died years ago."

"I don't know," Siama whispered, "but somehow, she lives."

Unprepared for all the emotions Siama's confirmation would unleash, Ameenah sank onto the chair behind her. She had not realized how much of her feelings she'd held back until Siama's simple words set them free. Inside, she felt grief for all the years they'd been apart, fear for what her mother must have endured, but above all, hope for the real chance to see her mother again. Beside her, Nasir did not let go, kneeling beside Ameenah as she cried.

From across the room, Siama walked towards the table, her hands trembling as they extended out, daring to touch the dress.

"She's alive," Ameenah whispered. "I can *feel* her. Can you hear it, Siama, the calling?"

Slowly Siama touched the seam of the shoulder and closed her eyes.

"Yes," she whispered. "I hear her."

Nasir leaned forward and skimmed his hand over the dress. He'd never seen a finer garment anywhere. But all he felt were threads beneath his fingers. No tinge of power. No current of energy. No sound of any kind.

"I hear nothing," he admitted, feeling strange and distant from his companions.

Siama opened her eyes and smiled.

"It is not meant for you. Fewa speaks in a language you cannot know. You must be born to it."

"Born a girl?"

"Yes, but more than that. You must be born of the line of Amalaki."

Ameenah looked at Siama, stunned by the woman's words.

"How do you know my mother was Amasiti?"

"Your mother *is* Amasiti," Siama corrected. "This magic is new. Your mother lives, Ameenah, and you must find her. She created this dress for you. She would not have done so without a reason. You must find out what it means."

"The Hir's emissary said that the finest seamstress in the palace made the dress," Nasir added. "She must be there somewhere."

"Then that is where you must go," Siama replied.

Bolstered by Siama's blessing and the rising hope in her heart, Ameenah stood up and wiped away her tears with the back of her hand.

"I will go to the celebration and find her."

Beside her, Nasir's face grew hard as stone.

"Wait, Ameenah! What if this is a trap to lure you to him? If he knows that the dressmaker is your mother, he could have given this to you because he knew you would recognize her work. If that's true, it means that he knows who you are and is pretend-ing he doesn't on purpose. I don't like this."

Ameenah could see the reason behind his words, but none of it mattered to her.

"I have to go, Nasir. I don't see another way."

"As the Hir's guest?"

"How else would I ever get into the palace?"

"I could take you," Nasir pleaded. "He is a dangerous man, Ameenah. I don't want you alone with him."

"Should I refuse him, then arrive with you in the dress he gave me?"

Nasir looked away, knowing the decision was not his to make. The idea was brazenly stupid to begin with, yet he could not accept the thought of Ameenah on the Hir's arm. Seeing the fear in his eyes, Ameenah reached out and took Nasir's face in her hands.

"Look at me." She waited until he turned to face her. "I can take care of myself. I'll be careful. I promise."

"All the noble families have been invited," he said with resig-nation. "At least let me accompany you there."

He let out a sigh of relief as Ameenah slowly nodded in agree-ment.

"There is powerful magic, protective magic within the dress that no one else can see."

Startled by her words, Ameenah and Nasir looked over to find Siama hovering both hands over the garment as if trying to feel its essence through the air. "It will help keep her safe," Siama added.

"Magic?" Nasir replied. "Magic died long ago." Ameenah stood beside him, lost in thought as she fingered the rough jewel at her neck.

Siama's eyes snapped open.

"No, Nasir," she warned. "Magic is still alive, waiting for the one who is finally worthy enough to wield it. We must all be ready."

We will see if you are worthy, the creature had said to her. Ameenah shivered, remembering the Sri's words in the forest.

"How do you know this? You've never spoken of this before," Ameenah asked Siama. *Does she know about the Sri? Would she believe me if I told her everything that's happened?* Sometime soon Ameenah knew she would ask her when they were alone.

"I know because I am of the line of Amalaki, though I never had your mother's gifts. Fewa entrusted you to me because it is the tradition of our sisterhood to raise each other's children as our own. But I never knew her secrets. Only she can give you the answers you seek."

Though Nasir did not believe in magic, he knew one thing for certain as he turned back to Ameenah.

"If you're going, I will go with you," Nasir said. Before Ameenah could protest, he added, "You may not be my guest, but I cannot let you go alone. I will be there to help. If what Siama believes is true, your mother may have been held captive in the palace for a very long time. We don't know what state she will be in or what you will be facing, but regardless of what happens, you will not be alone."

"If she is alive, I will find her," Ameenah replied. "This is my family, Nasir. It's worth the risk."

Nasir hugged her then, hoping beyond reason that she was right.

CHAPTER 15

The Road Back

FOR THE FIRST time in many years, Ameenah allowed herself to think of them.

The sound of her mother's voice as she sang in the yard while tending her garden. The boisterous rumble of her father's laugh whenever he would hear a joke that pleased him. As a child, Ameenah was accustomed to the constant flow of people in and around her home, so that she never feared the presence of strangers. People came from all over the city of Neema and beyond to seek out her mother's healing potions and ointments. Given that her father was next in line for the Governorship of Nor, and from a high-ranking noble family, it was highly unusual and often frowned upon for a woman of her class to work, let alone serve the people in such a way. But her mother insisted that a woman must always be true to her calling, no matter what society thought of her. Ameenah could never recall her father showing anything but pride towards the woman who bore his children. He called her Ami T'iru, (*my love*, in the ancient tongue) but never 'my wife', which was the custom throughout Yet.

For six years, Ameenah lived a life of luxury and happiness. As the youngest child in their family, Ameenah was doted on by her parents and shielded from every harm by her brother, Haveer.

Little did she know that beneath the facade of their peaceful life, revolution was brewing. As the people were taxed more and given less, resentment of the Hir grew. Skirmishes broke out between the Hir's guard and the people along the southern borders of Nor and Harat.

With the largest army and most plentiful resources, Nor's Simbu-Ki fought back hardest. They also bore the brunt of the Hir's cruelty as he tried to put down those who dared to fight against the excesses of his rule. Entire families were captured in the middle of the night, only to be found hanging from the clock towers in the cool breeze of morning.

Looking back, Ameenah realized that her mother knew their time was coming. In those final days, Fewa had been obsessed with beading Ameenah's hair, making her and Haveer their favorite treats, and singing them strange songs in a language Ameenah had never heard before.

Ameenah would never know how the Hir's men managed to slaughter all the soldiers who were sworn to protect her family, but when his soldiers came into her home just hours before dawn, her father was the first to die, defending his family. Her mother had tried to hide them, but Haveer refused, determined to avenge his father and protect his mother and sister. Ameenah remembered him as a gentle but serious boy of thirteen who wore his hair shorn just to avoid their mother's comb. Haveer's skill with a blade cost the Hir two soldiers, but it cost Ameenah much more as the soldiers finally overpowered him.

Terrified, Ameenah watched from the crease in a locked cabinet as her mother and brother were dragged away. When the night was silent again, Ameenah kicked open the door and found a knapsack with food, clothing, her mother's jewelry, and money waiting for her with a note in her mother's handwriting that read:

You are never truly alone.

Find Siama

The years that followed had been hard, filled with loneliness and doubt, but she had survived. More than that, she had learned to make a living, build a home, and defend it. She had taken everything she'd learned from her family—her father's quiet independence and unwavering integrity, her brother's fearless sense of adventure, and her mother's vision and determination—and created the life she had now. In this way, she kept them with her, so that she would never lose them completely.

But now she had another chance.

The mere thought that she might see her mother again, even for a moment, filled her with almost too much hope to bear.

In preparing for the celebration, Ameenah followed the rituals she watched her mother do a thousand times whenever she dressed for the day. Though she never reveled in it, Fewa was admired throughout the provinces for her beauty and style. Each day Fewa twisted and pinned her hair, then chose her clothing with meticulous care, as if every day was a magnificent event. She then donned her jewelry: bracelets, necklaces, rings, and even bangles on her ankles, so that she tinkled and shimmered everywhere she went.

Now, Ameenah did the same. She began with a bath filled with precious oils then combed the tangles from her hair and braiding it loosely with a ribbon made of blue silk. When she was done, Ameenah slipped into the dress her mother had made for her. It fit like a warm embrace. Last, Ameenah put on her mother's jewelry, all the jewelry her mother had saved for her in the knapsack that had been her lifeline. When Ameenah finally looked in the mirror, she gasped at the familiar sight. The woman in front of her looked almost exactly like the mother she remembered, and Ameenah was shocked to find herself beautiful. Secretly she hoped that Nasir would find her so as well.

No sooner had she thought his name did she hear him approaching. By carriage, the journey to Mera Meja took at least four hours on the best of roads. Since he hated to be late, Ameenah knew that Nasir would arrive well before then. Even though she would have to endure the Hir once she arrived at the celebration, at least she would have the trip to Kiveer with Nasir to calm her nerves and plan how she would slip away and find her mother.

Grabbing her mother's blue shawl, Ameenah stepped outside to see a carriage covered in crisp, creme linen and gold molding with the Sigil of Nor emblazoned on the door. It was stunning, but not nearly as beautiful as the man who emerged from within. In his usual armor, it was easy to forget that Nasir was royalty, a member of one of the oldest families in Yet.

But looking at him now it was unmistakable. Nasir's locks flowed loosely over his back and shoulders like thick jet-black ropes of coarse silk. His kaftan was long, a pristine cream with embroidered threads of blue and gold at the cuffs, hem, and collar. Underneath, the drape of his pants flowed gracefully to meet his blue slippers.

Across his chest lay a scarab of thickly woven gold and blue fabric that held his kaskara at his back. The sword was meant to be ceremonial, a sign of his rank as a military commander, but

Ameenah knew him too well. Nothing about Nasir was ornamental, everything with him had a purpose, and she knew the blade he carried was sharp.

They walked towards one another in silence, each awed by the sight of the other.

"*Ameenah,*" Nasir whispered as he reached for her jeweled hand. "You look..."

She smiled then, delighted by his genuine loss for words.

"Thank you," she said, reaching for his other hand. As she leaned up to kiss his cheek, the sound of another carriage caught her ears.

"It's just my family," Nasir said, refusing to look away from the curve at the center of her upper lip. "They were supposed to come with me, but they were taking too long. They promised to meet us here on time."

Ameenah stepped away. "It's not," she said breathlessly as the black and red exterior of the approaching carriage glinted through the trees. "It's one of the Hir's men."

Nasir whirled around in confusion. His family had already sent word to Mera Meja that Ameenah would be traveling with them to the palace. Sending a carriage to escort her was highly unusual under the circumstances, but he could still accompany her. He would gladly send his own carriage back for the chance to ride with her instead.

He did not anticipate that when the carriage came to a halt in front of them, the Hir himself would step out with a triumphant grin.

"Ameenah, you are a sight to behold," he said as he descended from his carriage. The Hir's eyes raked over her lustfully before Nasir stepped in front of Ameenah in a vain attempt to block his gaze.

"Nasir. How thoughtful of you to keep Ameenah from harm until I arrived."

"My family sent word, Ja Hir. I have come to escort her to the celebration."

"Well, as you can see, there is no need."

When Nasir made no attempt to move from between them, the Hir's eyes narrowed.

"If I didn't know better, I could almost be forgiven for thinking that you are attempting to deprive me of the pleasure of Ameenah's company on the long ride to Mera Meja."

Nasir stood still, fighting every instinct in his body that told him to reach for his sword and cut this treacherous man down. If he gave in to his impulses, Ameenah might never get the chance to find her mother and Nor would be at war with no allies willing to rally to their cause over such a small infraction.

But it didn't feel small to Nasir. To him, it felt like holding the darkness back from the light. No matter how hard he tried, he could not convince himself to move.

Just behind them, another carriage came into view. The Hir squinted with displeasure as he saw Nasir's family's carriage pull up beside his. The carriage barely had time to stop before Rahmeel and Nasir's father stepped out, anxious to allay the tension they could see easily from their carriage window.

"Ja Hir, what a surprise to find you here," Rahmeel said with a deep bow. Nasir watched his brother in shock. The Hir was not a king. Yet had no king. Walking past his eldest son, Jaleen came quietly to stand beside Nasir, placing a firm hand on his shoulder.

"We traveled here to take Ameenah to the celebration ourselves. We sent word of our intentions so that you would be spared the trouble of sending an escort or collecting her yourself. A host should never be so far away from his own party."

"Do not insult my guest, Sa Min Jaleen. To have such a woman as Ameenah in my possession could only be a pleasure."

Behind them Ameenah felt a sickening dread spread through her belly.

Four hours.

Alone.

With him.

The thought made her slightly dizzy with fear, but if all that was at stake was her physical safety, she would not be concerned. The leather sheath of her knife was pressed firmly to the inside of her thigh where she was sure she could get to it, if need be. Her fear stemmed from the sudden awareness that she would be willing to do anything, *endure* anything for the chance to achieve her only goal: to find her mother.

She stepped in front of Nasir, Rahmeel, and their father, knowing that there was no looking back.

"You honor me, Ja Hir," she began with a smile and a voice that was so sweet she barely recognized it. "I would be grateful for your escort if you would allow me a moment to secure my home. I will only linger a moment longer."

The Hir sighed in exasperation.

"Surely one of your farm hands can see to such things."

"The harvest is over, Ja Hir. All of my farm hands have gone save Opa, who is very ill," she replied, straining to keep the tension from her voice. In reality, Opa was completely healed and out of sight by her request, watching as the scene unfolded from his cabin along with two dozen men they'd hired to secure the farm with him while she was away.

"Then one of my men can help," he offered.

Again, Ameenah demurred. "I have no wish to trouble your guard or extend your kindness any further, Ja Hir, but I will not be settled until I see the task done myself. It will only take a moment."

Before the Hir could protest any further, Ameenah turned to Nasir.

"Would you help me lock the gates? I don't want my goats to wander while I'm away."

You don't have any goats, he thought before realizing, that was exactly her point.

Breaking away from his father's grip, Nasir followed her lead without a word until they were far enough that they could be sure no one would hear.

"I can't let you do this," he whispered as they made their way to the back fence.

"Think, Nasir! This could be my only chance to save her." Seeing the desperation in his eyes, she tried to speak calmly. "I won't be alone. You will follow close behind. He wouldn't try anything with so many people so close."

Nasir wanted to believe her, but he couldn't.

"Promise me you'll scream if he tries anything. Anything."

"I promise," she whispered. Together they secured the heavy back fence then returned to the carriage.

She found the Hir waiting for her anxiously as he fidgeted with something inside the folds of his robe.

Ameenah stepped forward. "Thank you for your patience, Ja Hir. I feel so much better knowing my home will be secure until I return."

She could feel Nasir's gaze boring into her as she took the hand the Hir offered, but she did not look back.

"Shall we?" the Hir purred, with eyes that shone with nefarious delight.

Ameenah did not look away from his gaze. Instead, she tightened the shawl around her neck and shoulders and stepped into the cavernous darkness of the Hir's carriage.

CHAPTER 16

Wet' 'Imedi

THE MOMENT HIS footman closed the carriage door, they were off. Inside, the curtains were closed so tightly that the only light between them came from two red candles that flickered from heavy wrought-iron sconces.

The Hir settled back in his seat, as if sitting on a throne. Ameenah thought she had never seen him look so serene or sure of his command of the situation before him. With arms stretched out on either side, his posture displayed the gold embroidery that accented his traditional black and red attire. In the confines of the carriage, his robes were so voluminous that his thin frame took up the entire seat.

"Finally, we are alone. For a girl who lives so deep in the forest, you certainly have a lot of friends."

In the close confines, his voice was darkly seductive like a shadow beckoning her closer. Though his skin clung tightly to the sharp bones underneath, its dark brown hue was smooth and flaw-less, without a trace of facial hair. With a few pounds added and a genuine smile, Ameenah could imagine how, in a certain light that masked the strange hollow of his eyes, one might mistake him for handsome.

"Sa Min Jaleen and his family have been kind to me," she replied, willing her breathing to remain calm.

"You've known them for a long time, then?" The Hir's eyes drifted away, suddenly interested in some imaginary thread on the hem of his sleeve.

"Since I was a child." When he did not react, Ameenah began to suspect that his line of questioning was more a test than an inquiry.

How much does he know about my mother, about me, she wondered.

"I see," he replied, with eyes kept low. "And how did a girl-child come to live alone, at the end of the world?"

Ameenah racked her brain for a lie that would justify the extreme life she'd chosen for herself, but nothing but the truth would suffice.

Well, perhaps not all of it, she thought. *He may be arrogant, but he's not a stupid man,* she warned herself. *Do not underestimate him.*

"My family was taken from me, murdered in the night. I've lived on my own ever since."

"Oh, I am sorry to hear of it. Those were dark times. Dark, dark times." The Hir returned his eyes to hers without a trace of remorse in his voice and, suddenly, she knew.

This is a trap, just as Nasir warned me it would be. He knows exactly who I am.

As if reading her mind, the Hir's veneer of gentility slipped just enough to reveal a knowing smirk.

Ameenah held her breath against the instinct to scream. Outside, she could not hear Nasir's carriage, but she hoped that he was close. *But not close enough to stop what I've already begun.*

The sweet scent of the burning candles, which at first had been only annoying, now made Ameenah's head throb with pain. The red wax crept down the sides of the sconces, making the entire display look like it was dripping with blood.

Ameenah closed her eyes against a sudden wave of nausea.

"Well, the important thing is that you're here now, isn't it? After all my searching, I've finally found you. And look how magnificent you are in that dress! I wondered if it would be worth all the trouble it took to make it. But I knew once you saw it you would not be able to refuse my invitation."

Ameenah's body felt flush and her throat hoarse with a sudden burning heat. The cloying scent of the candles made it more and more difficult for her to breathe.

"You seem uncomfortable, my dear. Quite the opposite of what I'd intended. Our carriage is large enough for you to lie down if you like."

Now he's toying with me, she thought, forcing her eyes open. *But I won't give in so easily.*

Her voice was low but clear as she answered him. "No, thank you, Ja Hir. It's just the scent of the candles. I find it a bit too sweet for my liking."

"That is a shame. I had them made especially for you." His lips smiled, but his eyes were piercing. Instinctively, Ameenah loosened the shawl from around her neck and clutched the amulet she always wore.

Help me, Ina. Help me.

"Might we open the window?" she asked, forcing herself to take slow, measured breaths. Around her the dress began to pulsate in a calming rhythm.

The Hir's eyes followed her grasp to the object around her neck. A short hiss escaped his lips as a flash of rage rippled across his face.

"My dear, what is that awful thing you're wearing around your neck?"

Ameenah watched his right hand disappear inside the folds of his clothes.

"It was my mother's," she said calmly, remembering what the Sri had told her. *He sees, but he cannot truly understand what it is.*

"What kind of mother would leave her daughter such an ugly thing? I'm afraid to say it simply will not do," the Hir cooed. His face began to relax as he brought a heavy gold link chain from a disguised pocket in his robe.

"I intended to give this to you upon my arrival, but your *guests* distracted me." The memory of their presence vexed him, but he would not let it keep him from his goal any longer.

Once she wears my chain.... he thought.

Ameenah closed her eyes and focused on the rhythm of the dress to fight back the dizziness that clouded her mind. Keeping her left hand clutched to the rough stone that had grown strangely warm beneath her skin, she used her right hand to reach under the window curtain. She pressed her palm firmly to the thin pane, reveling in the cool air that rushed past the glass. Instantly, she felt more focused. In the distance, she heard the sharp howl of a wolf.

The Hir inched forward in his seat as he watched sweat form on Ameenah's brow.

Why isn't it working, he seethed silently. His alchemist, Nafar, had promised that the candles would work as long as she had no access to the outside elements. *She must submit to me!* The Hir stood up.

"Take it off," he commanded, finally at the end of his patience.

When Ameenah opened her eyes, she was surprised to find him hunched over her in the carriage, reaching for her with a gold necklace in his hand.

"I can't," Ameenah replied. The jagged edges of the amulet cut into her palms, but still she held it close. Whether it burned with the heat of her own body or some unknown power, she could not say, but she would not let go.

"What makes you think you can defy me, girl?"

"I promised I would never take it off. I never have, and I never will."

The Hir examined the hideous necklace more carefully. *It's too crude to be an amulet of the Amasiti*, he decided before moving forward.

"We will see about that!" he snarled, reaching for her throat with the gold necklace in hand.

Without thinking, Ameenah swung her right hand from the windowpane and smacked his arm away from her.

The necklace flew from his hand, skidding across the carriage floor. Incensed, the Hir darted away to retrieve the necklace from the floor, then lunged at her throat again. The light from the candles burned in his eyes like madness. But, before he could reach her, the carriage suddenly jolted, throwing him back into his seat.

Outside, the air around them erupted with savage growls. The screams of the footmen behind them were followed by a loud crash. By the time they heard the footman scream again, his voice was an echo in the distance as their carriage raced away.

"Yeakob!" the Hir called to his driver. "What's happening?"

Despite the brief commotion and the eerie silence that followed, the driver did not stop or slow his pace.

Still clutching her necklace, Ameenah pressed her back against her seat, trying to stay as far away from the Hir as she could. A new danger was coming, but not for her.

With one hand anchored to the cushion for balance, the Hir used his other fist to bang on the carriage roof.

"Yeakob! Answer me! What the hell is going on?"

"I don't know, Ja Hir!" Yeakob stammered. "I think we may be under attack!"

"What do you mean 'may be'? Who would dare?" The Hir pulled back the curtain and opened the window.

Quickly, Ameenah slid to the other side of the carriage. With the necklace still wrapped between his fingers, the Hir pressed his hand against the window frame and leaned his head out.

At first, he could see nothing close to them in the vast plains that lay before the palace at Mera Meja. The only sound he heard in the darkness was the wheels of their carriage rattling along the road as the driver raced ahead. Once his eyes adjusted, in the distance, the Hir saw the faint outline of Nasir's family carriage, but they were too far behind to be of any consequence to his plans.

They're too late, he thought, remembering Nasir's feeble attempt to prevent Ameenah from traveling with him. *At least Jaleen is no fool. It doesn't matter now anyway. Soon we will be home and Ameenah will submit to me, one way or another.*

"What are you talking about?" the Hir yelled towards Yeakob. "There's nothing out here!"

From inside the carriage Ameenah heard the sound of large claws drawing back against the polished wood top of the carriage. From the sudden turn of his head, Ameenah could see that the Hir heard it as well, but not soon enough to save him. He looked up to find the large face of a tan wolf growling down at him.

The attack came from two sides. Frozen in terror at the presence of the first wolf, he did not see the second lean in from behind the carriage to bite his hand, taking two fingers and the necklace they held with it. For a moment, the Hir forgot about the wolf above his head, staring in disbelief at his ravaged hand. But he remembered, just in time to meet the paw that came down to scrape its claw across the side of his face. Pain finally found its voice as the force of the blow knocked him to the carriage floor, bleeding and wounded at Ameenah's feet.

Without a thought, Ameenah reached for the door, ready to jump out of the moving carriage until a thought stayed her hand.

If I leave now, how will I find her? Even as the Hir's prisoner, Ameenah knew she had a better chance of finding her mother than if she were anywhere else.

Atop the carriage, Ameenah could hear the anxious scratching of wolf's claws, *her* wolf's claws, against the roof as he howled.

Suddenly, she understood. *He's beckoning me, beckoning me to come with him.*

I can't, she thought. *There is something I must do.* As soon as she made the decision, Ameenah felt the carriage pass from soft dirt to the paved stone of the long palace driveway and knew no matter what happened, there was no going back.

Outside, the palace guards shouted as they raced towards their liege. "Wolves! The Hir is under attack. Shoot them down!"

Run, she thought. *Run away before they catch you.* The wolf howled again and this time she knew he understood her.

Go! she commanded, then felt the carriage rock with the force of two wolves leaping off and away.

Behind her, the Hir whimpered and cursed. In the time she'd decided not to escape, he had managed to roll on his knees and wrap his torn hand in the fabric from his robe. From his crouch, he glared at her. Fury mixed with the blood and torn flesh that ran down his face. But there was also a wild excitement, too, and a lust in his eyes that made Ameenah's skin crawl.

"Did you send them?" he asked. His voice was strained with pain.

Though Ameenah knew the answer, she refused to say the words out loud.

She had not sent them. Yet, somehow they had come. They had come *for her*. Just as they had during the bandits' attacks. They had sensed she was in danger and came to save her. Though she still did not understand why, Ameenah could not deny the strange connection anymore.

As if taken by some fit of madness, the Hir suddenly began to howl at her mockingly, before descending into laughter.

The moment the carriage driver pulled up the horses, the Hir's guardsmen opened the door to find their leader maimed and bloody, with Ameenah unharmed beside him. And no matter how she felt, no one could save her from the path she'd chosen.

"Well, there is no one here to save you now." The Hir's sneer was grotesque as blood ran

down his teeth and out the side of his ruined mouth.

But Ameenah could not look away because, for once, she knew he was right.

CHAPTER 17

Mera Meja

"LOCK HER IN my chambers!" the Hir roared from the carriage floor.

Without warning, two palace guards who were twice her size stepped forward to pull her from the carriage. Despite their roughness, Ameenah did not struggle. She didn't want to give them any excuse to bind her hands. It would only make it more difficult to escape wherever they were taking her.

Once secured within their grasp, Ameenah looked up from her captors to find herself at the center of attention. The Hir's carriage had stopped at the opening of an enormous circular driveway with stone pillars that framed the entrance to the palace. Before her stood thousands of people, servants in crisp tan uniforms fluttering between dignitaries and guests dressed in the finest attire Ameenah had ever seen. Large, brilliant feathers floated in the air, perched atop bright turbans and head wraps to make each head-dress more dramatic than the last. Jewels sparkled, not only around the necks and wrists of the women, but on the sleeves and colors of the men as well, displaying their wealth as a sign that they had earned the right to be in the presence of the Hir.

As she took them in, all eyes were on the spectacle of Ameenah, dressed like a guest yet treated like a prisoner. Oblivious to the attention, the guards hustled her through the crowd that stood outside the main palace entrance, where all the most important guests arrived.

"Make way!" the guards called as each kept a firm grip on her arms. Ameenah could only imagine what she must look like compared to the other guests in their finery: hair disheveled, shawl askew, and slippers left in the carriage or lost somewhere on the long driveway that led up the stairs to the receiving area with its towering doors made of cedar and bronze.

An unsettled quiet came over the guests as she passed, but gestures and stares were the least of her concerns. Once she reached the top of the stairs, Ameenah was stunned by the enormity of what lay before her. She remembered the palaces in Nor from her childhood. They were beautiful homes with marble floors and towers that seemed to touch the sky. In her memory, she could not have imagined anything grander. Now she knew her imagination had been woefully inadequate.

The Palace of Mera Meja was more like a city with palaces upon palaces within, each more spectacular than anything she'd ever seen.

The city before her went on without any end that she could see, save the faint border of trees in the distance. Ameenah's heart sank as she realized that it might take her weeks, if not longer, to understand the layout of the palace before she had any hope of finding what she came for.

How will I ever find her? she wondered in despair before a commotion behind drew her attention.

At the far end of the palace road, a carriage raced into the driveway with a speed that threatened to plow through anyone that stood in its way. Until, at the last moment, the chargers that pulled the carriage reared, then crashed down in front of the startled crowd.

Ameenah turned, beckoned by the gasps and shrieks of the crowd, to see the runaway carriage door swing open and Nasir emerge before the horses had a chance to settle.

With his body leaning precariously past the doorframe, Nasir's neck craned in every direction, searching frantically, until he spotted her in the archway, being dragged up the steps by two guards. The look between them was brief, but it carried with it the full weight of all their failed plans before he watched her disappear into the palace.

Ameenah walked in silence. As the bustling sounds from the palace entrance faded away, she counted steps and memorized landmarks, anything she could use as a reference to navigate.

The palace doors opened to a large courtyard where the festivities for the anniversary were well underway. And to her surprise, the path to wherever the guards were taking her plunged Ameenah right through the middle of the celebration.

Revelers from every province paraded their finest attire as they danced and strutted around the vast open courtyard that was situated in the middle of the large complex that made up the first series of buildings in the palace. Musicians and entertainers of every kind were stationed along the borders of the courtyard so that wherever you turned, one could find something spectacular to capture their attention. Large trays of food and drinks hovered above the crowd, carried by sturdy hands that lowered and raised them with ease to satisfy the fancy of each guest. At the center of the courtyard was a large fountain that gave off the distinctive iridescent glow of the poisonous Cocau fish. If Ameenah had not been so focused on preserving her life, she would have marveled at the sheer spectacle before her.

On either side of the courtyard stood a pair of two-story buildings. From the open design on each level, she could see a series of closed doors made from redwood and black oak. The rooms extended along the length of the courtyard on two sides. On the second floor terrace of each building, the Hir's guards stood at every column watching the crowd.

Ameenah barely had time to guess their purpose before she was pushed towards the large archway. Once inside, the sound behind her seemed to vanish. In front of her, the pathway led to a stone bridge that flowed into a dome-shaped structure. In the dim light of the setting sun, Ameenah scanned the layout of the grounds, always looking for an escape. But all she could make out was the outline of several smaller buildings on either side of the bridge. Underneath, a dark pool rippled with a strange rhythm that both beguiled and frightened her.

Before she could guess what caused the pool to churn so strangely, she was pulled through another set of doors. The interior of the next palace was even more opulent, with marble, ancient art, and tapestries dyed in the most vibrant Pearl Rose colors Ameenah had ever seen. But, there was also an air of coldness to the decor. Torn, broken shapes of silver, copper, iron, and gold sat on pedestals along the hallways as if they had been ripped straight from the earth without polish or refinement.

Unlike the bright openness of the courtyard, the interior palace felt almost cavernous with its high ceilings, dark woods, and even darker decor. From the few open doors that Ameenah could see into, she glimpsed vast meeting rooms with tables almost as large as the Sparrow trees from which they were made. But she could not make out anything more. The rest of the walk was a blur as the guards rushed her up two flights of stairs, threw her into a room with no lights and closed the door tightly behind them.

"God help that girl if she had anything to do with bloodying the Hir," one of the guards said before retreating back down the hall.

At first, Ameenah stayed on the ground, pressing her fingers into the cool stone beneath her until her heartbreak was steady, then she waited. The second moon was rising high in the sky, with the third moon barely visible on the horizon.

I don't need the light to see, she reminded herself. It was finally night, when she felt her most alert. Her most powerful. Slowly, Ameenah got up from the floor and turned around, letting her eyes adjust to the darkness.

There was a large bed in front of her with two chairs that were shoved into the far corners at the front of the room. As her eyes adjusted, she could see that the bed was encased by a strange lattice around the tops and sides. As she reached out to touch it, her fingertips met the cold feel of metal. Absently, she wondered why anyone would want to sleep surrounded by metal, then refused to waste anymore time thinking about it.

Ameenah made her way to the bedroom's balcony, hoping she wasn't too far up to climb down. The distance to the ground shocked her. The two flights of stairs she climbed to get to the

Hir's chambers didn't strike her as especially steep, but she doubted she could find anything that would be long enough to see her down safely.

She looked across the landscape beneath her, trying to imagine where her mother might be. Every so often a building seemed to pop up without any pathway to it, each looking like islands floating in a sea of dark green grass.

Slowly, her mind traced back to the smaller arched corridors she'd seen on either side of the interior palace staircase. They had seemed to slope downward, but with no time for more than a fleeting glance, Ameenah wasn't sure if they were merely a staircase to a lower level or a tunnel of some kind. Either way, she was sure the passage between buildings was hidden underground, and if she wanted to find her mother, that was where she needed to go. All she needed to do was find a way out of the Hir's bedchambers.

After jiggling the handle and banging on the door to no avail, Ameenah began looking for a key in every drawer she could find. To her, the Hir seemed to be a man who insisted on being in control of everything. She could not imagine him being resigned to a room where he could be confined with no means of escape.

At first, she tried to be neat, slowly rifling through his things only to set them back where she found them. But the more time she spent looking for a key that she couldn't find, the less careful she was. Within minutes the pristine bedroom looked like a hyena had gotten loose within its confines and wreaked havoc. Ameenah could not find it within herself to care. If she couldn't escape before the Hir came back to find her, the mess she made would be the least of her worries.

After nearly an hour of scouring every surface within reach, she had not found anything that could help her escape. Frustrated and sweaty, she collapsed against a wall. Sliding to the floor on weary limbs, Ameenah closed her eyes and fought the tide of rising panic once again.

If I give in to this fear, I'll never find her, she pleaded with herself.

She had thought herself brave for so long, living at the edge of the world. *How stupid I've been. All this time, all I've ever done was guard my own safety.*

Here. Now. Fighting my way out of the mouth of a lion, this is where I must find courage. This is what it means to be brave.

Except now she knew she wasn't.

It's barely been an hour and I'm already on my knees.

Slowly, Ameenah reached for the stone that hung around her neck.

Help me, Ina. Help me find you.

Ameenah swallowed the salty taste of her own frailty and wiped away her tears. Resolved to try climbing down the balcony, she placed her hands on the floor to push herself up when a stream of cool air running along her fingertips caught her attention.

From where she sat, pressed against the back wall at the farthest point from the terrace, the slight but steady stream of air made no sense to her. Still, curiosity and no better plan made her follow it. She crawled along the floor, tracing the airflow with her fingertips until she came to a seam in the wall.

Her heart thrummed with excitement. *Praise the Mother! Somewhere there is a secret doorway. Now, all I have to do is find it.*

But her joy was short-lived. Ameenah sprung to her feet as she heard the sound of raised voices coming down the hall.

"These are the Hir's private quarters. You don't belong here," she heard one of the Hir's guards say. The voice that responded was muffled but prolonged.

Whoever it is, she thought, *they're not giving up easily.*

Ameenah had no idea what the outcome of the exchange would be, nor did she have any intention of waiting around to find out. Her hands shook as they skimmed the surface of the wall, looking for the opening, until finally she found a lever at the edge of the baseboard by the bed.

She hesitated for only a moment before she stepped on the flat metal latch. A smooth panel made of wood and painted plaster popped open and slid to the left. The draft she'd felt before gave way to a low howl as the air from the room sucked down the narrow stairway of a hidden tunnel.

A trembling hope welled up inside her as she placed her foot on the first stone step. Farther down the tunnel, she could see a low flickering light. More certain of her way, Ameenah turned around, looking for a way to close the secret panel behind her when the light from the hall that shown underneath the bedroom door suddenly became obscured by a pair of large feet.

Ameenah stepped back so quickly she almost lost her balance before bracing herself against the tunnel wall and slamming her shoulder onto a sharp lever beside the staircase. She watched long enough to see the Hir's chamber door handle jiggle then open as the secret door slid back into place. By the time she heard the screams of the guards, Ameenah was halfway down the staircase. She ran until she couldn't run anymore.

Nasir was beside himself. As a man of action, he was used to making a plan and seeing it through. He and Ameenah had that in common. His plan had been to take her to the palace and present her to the Hir. From inside the celebration, he and Kiva would watch their every move, making sure she was safe until his father, brother, and the other governors petitioned the Hir for a private audience. Ameenah would excuse herself, claiming to need the lavatory. Kiva would escort her out and back to him, where they would break away and search for Ameenah's mother together. That was the plan.

Until *he* arrived and took her. Until Nasir's father insisted that they take the slower, more luxurious family carriage to Mera Meja together, so that Jaleen could keep his youngest son under control despite Nasir's desire to take Tewa and follow the Hir's carriage himself.

Until the wolves came.

Until the guards met the Hir's carriage at the palace gates and swept her away before Nasir's family arrived.

The look of sheer terror in her eyes when she met his gaze across the crowded entrance pierced his soul. His only comfort was that the Hir was not with her. Nasir held her gaze until she was swallowed up by the crowd, then turned back to the carriage that delivered them in time to see another set of guards hastening to carry a badly-wounded and bloody Hir away from prying eyes.

Stunned, Nasir's first assumption was to wonder if Ameenah had dared to cause the Hir such harm, but the thought quickly left his mind. She would not have attacked him at the risk of losing the chance to see her mother. And if she had, his guards would have killed her by now.

Then, with a shiver, he remembered the wolves. Kiva told him during their carriage ride to the palace how they had saved Ameenah during the raid at her farm. He didn't understand it, but he suspected that they were the only reason that Ameenah had arrived unharmed.

Wherever Ameenah was now, he knew she was fighting to get away from whoever held her captive and Nasir had a new plan—to find her.

CHAPTER 18

The Dark Path

THE COLD, DAMP air rose to meet Ameenah the farther down she went, until finally the tunnel emptied into a large cavern that split into two paths. With no idea which way to go, Ameenah closed her eyes and listened for the voice that had been calling to her ever since she first touched the dress. Instantly, she felt the fabric pull tightly around her body, flooding her mind with images, words, songs, dances—memories that were not her own, and underneath, a language she did not know.

Yet, somehow, Ameenah understood.

In her mind, she saw an image of a woman's frail, withered hands pulling golden thread through a needle. The hands worked quickly, tying off a knot before returning to their work—a golden dress. *Her* dress. Ameenah watched in awe as the thread shimmered then disappeared into the fabric, with every turn of her needle making it more brilliant than when she began. The woman's hair draped over her shoulders and onto the table in dirty, uneven curls. Ameenah could not see her face, but she had no doubt who the woman was.

Clutching her mother's necklace, she searched her vision for any clue that would tell her which way to go. Ameenah saw thick mudstone walls that were curved like where she stood, but lower. Rusted bars confined her mother in the small space that looked like it had been her home for a very long time.

Instinctively, Ameenah opened her eyes, turned left and ran. Along the way, she tried to catalog any landmarks that might hint to where she was or how she might find her way back, but there was almost nothing. Worse, the cavern was littered with other pathways and tunnels that looked identical to the one on which she traveled. Torches lit the way every fifty feet, which allowed her just enough light to see her feet in front of her but gave no warning of anyone or anything that could be lurking in the shadows.

The farther she ran, the deeper the cold crept into her bones. With no end to the tunnel in sight, Ameenah began to worry that she could get lost in its depths for weeks without ever finding her mother.

Her fear of wandering aimlessly through the palace's underground maze was interrupted by the sound of clinking armor approaching from behind. Ameenah darted into the first tunnel she could reach.

Within the main tunnel, palace guards Neveen Wor and his twin brother Cyrus ambled through the foreboding dark with one torchlight between them.

"I hate coming down here," Cyrus grumbled.

"Yeah, we should be at the festival with everyone else. It's our celebration, too," Neveen huffed.

"The only people who come down here are the ones who never make it back out," Cyrus added.

The brothers laughed nervously before Neveen whispered, "I heard the Hir has strange meetings down here. Sometimes, they say you can hear the screaming and chanting all the way in the courtyard. I wouldn't want to be down here for that!"

"Now you're just trying to scare me," Cyrus replied. "Come on. Let's hurry up and finish our rounds. There's nothing down here anyway."

Naveen and Cyrus continued down the darkened path and out of sight, but Ameenah waited a while before inching her way back towards the main tunnel. Once she reached the edge, Ameenah poked her head out, listening carefully until she was sure she couldn't hear the guards anymore. She leaned forward, preparing to move when suddenly someone grabbed her waist from behind and put a large hand over her mouth.

Ameenah went rigid against the man behind her, ready to scream before strong hands turned her to face him.

Relief washed over her as she saw Nasir's face only inches from her own.

"Sshhh!"

The scent of his cologne surrounded her, calming her racing heart. Slowly, Nasir withdrew his hand from around her mouth, then crushed her body to his.

"Are you all right?" he whispered as he tried to pull away and get a better look at her face, but Ameenah would not let him go.

"Yes," Ameenah replied. "They locked me in his bedchambers, but I found a secret passage and got away."

Nasir inched back from her then, just enough so that Ameenah could see his eyes beaming with relief and pride.

"How did you find me?" she asked, just as relieved to see him.

"After I lost you in the crowd, I followed the Hir and his men. I figured he would lead me to you."

"I haven't seen him since the carriage."

"I know." It was then that Ameenah saw the fear in Nasir's eyes.

"What is it? What did you find?"

"We're too late, Ameenah. While we've been trying to keep peace, the Hir has been gathering allies to overthrow us. Armies from outside our border have joined forces with him to seize control of the provinces and take the country for himself. He plans to take ownership of the land and everyone on it. Everything I feared is true."

"How do you know this?"

"I heard them plotting with my own ears. When I followed him, after they summoned a healer to bandage his hand, they took him straight to a room where generals from four countries—some as far away as Mohab and Zar—were waiting for him. They said that all their armies are ready to march on Yet as soon as the Hir gives the order."

Nasir hesitated, looking at Ameenah strangely before continuing. "The Hir said that an ally from within Yet had delivered a powerful weapon that will crush any resistance they encounter."

Ameenah felt her stomach turn cold.

"What weapon?"

"I don't know," Nasir replied. "The Hir said he still had to test its power, but that when he had mastered it, he would be unstoppable."

"How long? How long before he controls this weapon?"

Nasir shook his head. "All I know is we have no time. The Hir has been using these raids to distract and scatter our forces.

There is someone we can't trust among our allies, someone who has already betrayed us."

Determined, Nasir grabbed Ameenah's hand.

"We need to leave this place. I need to find my father and tell him."

Nasir stepped out of the shadows just as Ameenah jerked her hand away.

"I have to find my mother."

Nasir's eyes darted around the maze of tunnels in desperation.

"We don't know where she is, Ameenah. We can't risk..."

Ameenah shook her head, unyielding.

"She is the reason we are here! She is the reason that you discovered the Hir's plans. I won't leave this place without her."

Despite the danger of lingering, Nasir knew that Ameenah was right. He also knew that even if she wasn't, there was no dissuading her from continuing her search.

"I understand, I do. But how will we find her in all of this?" he asked. "There are too many pathways."

"You gather your family. I will find her, then meet you back here."

Nasir nodded, knowing that there was nothing he could do to change her mind.

"How will you find her?"

"I don't know," she answered honestly. "But I will."

"Ameenah!" he cried, exasperation growing in his voice.

"Trust me!"

Nasir grabbed both of her hands and squeezed, pushing his protection, his prayers, his love onto her like a shield.

"We will meet back here."

Ameenah nodded, meeting Nasir's piercing gaze with all the hope and determination she felt inside. His fear and his love for her were so clear, Ameenah could feel the tears rising, threatening to weaken her courage, but before she could let that happen, she tore herself away, clutched her necklace, and ran into the darkness of the tunnel.

CHAPTER 19

Ina

WITH EACH STEP Ameenah took, she doubted herself. She'd run so deep into the tunnel that there was almost no light. Whoever traveled this far into the labyrinth of the palace was clearly expected to bring their own torch to light their way. Ameenah had traveled ten minutes in utter darkness before she realized this and had to run back to retrieve the last torch she had passed on the wall.

But even with the torch in hand, the cold and the darkness closed in, sapping her courage and stealing her calm. The floor sloped downward, but beyond that she had no sense of where she was. After walking for almost thirty minutes, Ameenah was about to turn back when she heard a low moan. Startled by the sound, she peered deeper into the darkness until she could just make out the entrance to another tunnel.

There was no sign of anything beyond the darkness until she heard the soft rustling of chains. Certain that the sound came from within the new tunnel, she stepped forward and slipped over a small jagged step. After steadying herself, she followed the narrow staircase down, taking tiny steps with her hand braced against the rough stone wall. When she reached the bottom, her breath caught in her throat.

The stench of stale filth in the air was so overwhelming that she covered her mouth and nose with the palm of her hand to keep from gagging. After placing her torch in a sconce at the end of the staircase, she looked around. The cavernous room was constructed with the same rough stone as the staircase with a curved, low ceiling. Within, there were two rows of four cage-like cells. Ameenah counted four prisoners who looked like they were as old and weary as the prison that held them.

On the right, three cells were occupied with bodies hunched and folded on the ground. All the cells on the left were empty, except for the farthest one, where a lone prisoner kneeled with their back to the door. Because each prisoner wore the same sackcloth clothing and had hair that was long and matted, it was hard for Ameenah to determine if the prisoners were men or women. Stepping closer, she looked at the hands she could see.

One, maybe two women, she guessed.

Anxiously, Ameenah walked deeper into the cavern. Though her ears were tuned to the low whimpers and heavy breathing of the three prisoners to the right, her eyes were fixed on the motionless figure to the left who did not move or look her way as the others began to stir around her.

"Water! We need water. It's been days. Have mercy!"

Ameenah stepped toward the first man on her right. From the smoothness of the left side of his face, Ameenah could tell he had been handsome before whoever got a hold of him and burnt the entire right side of his face into a twisted mask of scarred skin. She looked around, trying to find anything that might be a source of water for the man.

"I'm sorry," she said after her search proved fruitless. " There is nothing here."

"Thank you. Thank you for trying," he murmured as if stung by her kindness then rolled back into a ball on the filthy floor.

Beside him was a girl, younger than Ameenah. The girl looked at Ameenah with wonder in her eyes but said nothing. Beside her a man hobbled to his feet as she approached and began to dance. His feet moved silently against the stone floor as he lifted his arms and swayed them from left to right.

"Have you come for me to try again?" he asked with an anxious smile and a mouth full of broken teeth. "I can do the dance for the Master. Better than she could. I swear!"

Ameenah backed away from the madness in his eyes, turning to the only prisoner she had yet to look upon.

In the last cell on the left side of the miserable hovel, Ameenah found her mother.

Fewa's legs were folded and facing sideways as she knelt on the floor. The sight of her was like looking into a broken mirror. Stunned, Ameenah fell to the ground outside her cell.

"Ina!"

Her mother did not turn to meet her gaze. She did not move at all from her place on the floor.

Reaching through the rusted bars with tears in her eyes, Ameenah whispered, "Ina, it's me, Ameenah . I have found you!"

Fewa barely reacted, blinking her eyes as she stared into the corner.

"Ina, it's me! Don't you remember me?"

"She don't talk, not anymore. Not since she made the dress. The one you wear."

Ameenah turned towards the only other female prisoner.

"What do you mean?"

"She worked on that dress like a fever that won't break. All day. All night. She was chanting and singing into that dress until she barely had a voice. She worked until the Hir's men came and tore the last stitch from her hands. She's not been the same since, like she poured the last bit of whatever she was into it. They say she was the only one to last so long with the Hir. She was so strong. So strong."

Ameenah was speechless with the knowledge that her mother had somehow broken herself to make this gift for her.

Why? she wondered to herself. *After all these years, how could she think I would want anything more than her?*

"Why would she take herself away from me just to give me this?"

Sensing Ameenah's grief, the girl moved forward. "Don't be sad," she said. "It's such a pretty dress. I think she must have really wanted you to have it."

As the girl leaned forward, the bars to her cell door creaked open. At first, Ameenah could not comprehend what she was seeing until she realized that all of the cell doors were unlocked.

The woman's eyes went wide with terror as her hands flew up to pull the bars back in place.

"Please don't tell," she cried, scurrying to the back of her cell.

"Why don't you free yourself?" Ameenah asked, a new type of dread twisting her heart.

"He tried to free himself," the woman answered, nodding to the half-burnt man to her left. "I tried to tell him. Now he knows. There is no escape."

Beside the girl, the dancing man swung his arms wildly.

"See, I know the dance. Please let me try again," he cried, but Ameenah couldn't stand to be in this place any longer.

Ameenah turned back to her mother, opened the bars that no longer separated them, and stepped inside.

Her mother made no acknowledgment of Ameenah's presence as she knelt in front of her. A mix of heartbreak and anger washed over Fewa's daughter as she took in the state of the woman she had adored all her life. In all her memories, she could not recall her mother ever being so disheveled. Even at bedtime her mother's thick coils had been neatly braided, her body clean, oiled, and perfumed.

Now, Fewa's hair was matted and grey with sprigs of unkempt curls sprouting out at every angle. Her dress was a lifeless brown with no trace of the flare for which her mother had been known. But the beauty of her face, despite the smudges of dirt and the creases along her forehead and eyes, remained. And when Ameenah ducked down to see her face fully, she was amazed to find a whisper of a smile on her full, cracked lips. It was Fewa's expression that finally broke Ameenah's heart and brought her tears tumbling down, for now she was certain that the mother she knew, the mother she'd held so dear, no longer existed.

But nothing could stop her from trying one last time. Gently, Ameenah took her mother's face in her hands.

"Ina, please. It's Ameenah, your daughter. Don't you remember?"

Slowly, Fewa raised her eyes to meet Ameenah's. Her expression was kind, but there was no indication that her mother had any idea who she was. The distance of all the years they'd been apart hit Ameenah like a blow to her chest. How many times had she dreamt about her mother, wishing that she was near, to love and guide her? Now she had everything she'd wished for between the palms of her hands, but even after all this time, her mother was still gone, as far away from her now as she had been in all her dreams.

"A daughter of Amalaki should have no reason to cry," Fewa said as she reached up to wipe Ameenah's cheek. Though her mother's hands were rough and dirty, her touch was gentle, just as Ameenah remembered. The sound of her mother's voice that had been locked beyond memory for so long suddenly came rushing back. Ameenah was so stunned by the sound, she almost couldn't understand her.

"What?" she asked, giddy and dumfounded all at once.

"You are of the Amasiti, yes?"

"I... I don't know," Ameenah replied.

"There can be no mistake, child. My eyes are not so old that they have forgotten magic." Slowly, Fewa's hands drifted down to Ameenah's neck and hovered over the jewel of the necklace. Ameenah held her breath and hoped.

"Oh yes, you wear the mark as one who was born to it, but this is not yours."

"How do you know that?" Ameenah whispered.

"Because it hides its magic, even from you. There would be no need to do so if it was yours. Who gave it to you?"

The answer stuck in Ameenah's throat. The woman before her was clearly fragile.

Could she bear the truth if I told it?

"My mother gave it to me," Ameenah answered finally. "She made me swear never to take it off."

"Your mother was wise," Fewa said, her hand falling back to her lap. "It will protect you from prying eyes, *evil* eyes. This is not a safe place."

"That's why I'm here. I've come to take you home."

Fewa met her gaze again and smiled.

"Sweet child, I will die here, but you must go. Your time does not end here. Your time has just begun."

Ameenah shook her head, fighting back new tears.

"No! I've just found you. I won't let anyone take you from me again."

"No one takes me!" Fewa said with a force that seemed as effortless and immovable as the earth itself. "I alone choose."

Confused, Ameenah remembered the unlocked gate and the unguarded passage.

"Then why have you stayed here so long if you could have escaped?"

"Escape?" Fewa looked at Ameenah as if the idea had never occurred to her before. This was not the mother she remembered.

Fewa continued, "There was something I had to do. Something I had to give away to serve her, but now I can't remember. I held onto everything I'd learned for so long, but now I have given all my secrets away."

"Why, Ina? I don't understand. How could a mother stay away from her child?"

Fewa turned to her with a frown. "If I had a daughter like you I would do anything to protect her. It would be nothing to stay here forever to keep her hidden, to keep her safe."

"I am safe," Ameenah replied, choking down the weight of her own grief to receive the gift her mother had provided all these years.

"Yes, I see that, but it is not enough. You still don't know who you are. The magic is hidden from you."

"What magic? Listen to me, Ina, we must leave this place." Ameenah shifted, preparing to stand, but her mother grabbed her hand, holding her in place.

"Where…" Fewa's voice faded as her eyes darted around the room confused and frightened, as if she'd been awakened from the middle of a dream. Sharply, her eyes turned to Ameenah, as if registering her presence for the first time. "You cannot be here! This is a terrible place."

"I know," Ameenah replied, unsure of what had suddenly agitated her mother. "That's why we're leaving."

Slowly, Ameenah lifted her mother to her feet and sighed with relief to find her physically stronger than she'd expected. Together, they walked out of the cell to the bottom of the staircase. Ameenah looked back to find the other prisoners shaking their heads with expressions of grave warning.

Come with us, she wanted to say even though she knew they would not.

"He will not let you leave," the girl cried frantically as they took their first steps up the stairwell.

"They all die!" the young woman yelled again as Ameenah and her mother continued to climb.

"They all die!"

CHAPTER 20

The Place of No Return

THE TORCH WENT out halfway into their climb, but Ameenah lead the way, ignoring the echoes of warning behind them.

When they made it to the top of the stairs, Ameenah turned right. With her mother tucked securely at her side, she needed no light to guide her way. She simply followed the sound of the quarreling voices that beckoned from the far side of the tunnel.

"I want Fewa to be alive, too, Nasir, but what are the chances?" Nasir's mother Medi's voice was low but insistent. "I knew Fewa. If there was a chance that she could have made it home, she would have by now."

"We could be lost down here for ages before any of the Hir's guards find us," Jaleen added. "We should go back and find your brother."

"No!" Nasir insisted. "Siama agreed. No one else could have made the dress. She will come back."

"It doesn't matter," Kiva added, slightly out of breath as she ran up to stand beside her brother. "You heard Nasir. We can't go back and risk the Hir's guards finding us. And we're *not* leaving without Ameenah. I found another way out through a tunnel over there."

"And what of your brother? You would leave Rahmeel here alone?" Medi asked.

"Rahmeel will find a way to take care of himself," Kiva replied. "He always does."

Afraid of adding more noise to their loud whispers, Ameenah held her mother close as they crept towards the voices of Nasir's family. Though they were close enough that the sound of their quarrel carried in the cavernous place, they were not so near that Ameenah would risk calling out.

From close behind, her mother whispered, "Who are those people?"

Ameenah turned to her and answered. "They are friends."

"Are you sure?"

Ameenah held her mother's hand tighter and moved forward, unable to find the words to reassure her. Regardless of what his family might say, Ameenah knew she could trust Nasir and Kiva with her life. There was no going back. Whatever danger lay ahead, they would have to face it together.

When Ameenah drew close enough to hear the dirt crunch under their restless feet, she decided to call out.

"Nasir?"

"Just in front of you. We're here."

Holding her mother, Ameenah stepped out of the shadows and into the glow of Nasir's torchlight. His parents gasped at their first glimpse of Fewa.

"Is it really you, Fewa, after all these years?" Medi asked.

Fewa stared back at them with skeptical eyes but did not answer. Nothing was familiar to her. Nothing but the girl by her side and the necklace around her neck.

"She doesn't remember," was all Ameenah could say in response to their confused expressions.

Seeing the grief and sadness in Ameenah's eyes, Nasir placed his hand on her shoulder to comfort her.

"All that matters now is that she is with us," he replied.

"We need to leave," Kiva announced. Nasir handed her the lone torch and nodded for her to lead them. "This way. Place your hand along the wall," Kiva ordered. "And watch your step."

As soon as they stepped into the tunnel, they could hear the wind growing loud and harsh as they followed. Unlike the previous passages they'd taken, the floor of this tunnel was unpaved with shallow ditches on either side of the path and sharp edges all along the walls.

At the back of their party, Ameenah held her mother with one hand and her dagger with the other as they walked, feeling the wind grow wild in the narrow space.

Suddenly, a light illuminated a narrow metal grate.

Fueled by the dim light and the certain possibility of escape, Nasir and Kiva rushed forward.

"What are we going to do about this lock?" he asked just before Kiva began kicking the gate. With an exasperated expression, Nasir extended his hand to keep Kiva back. He examined the door. It looked like no one had used it in a thousand years. Rusted and weather-worn, Nasir wondered what its original purpose had been in the first place. The lock looked even worse, ready to open with the right incentive. He turned to Kiva.

"Find me a rock, as big as you can."

Immediately, Kiva began scanning the ground as Nasir reached behind his back for his sword. He wrapped the handle in his waist sash and began pummeling the lock, but after several tries, he still couldn't get the leverage he needed for a clean strike.

"Here! Try this," Kiva said, handing him a large, oval-shaped stone. It only took three tries to break the lock clean off.

Nasir pulled back the lever and opened the gate, moving aside to let his family and Ameenah slip past.

They stepped out into a large open field with a jagged cliff just ahead of them. Though Nasir's family had been to the palace many times, he'd never seen this place before, never knew this place even existed. With no one in their immediate sight, Nasir risked a small sigh of relief, pulling in air that tasted sour on his tongue despite the steady breeze and crisp night air.

In the distance, they could hear the revelry still underway at the palace. Briefly, Nasir wondered how long it would take for all their merriment to turn to sorrow. He couldn't afford to dwell on any of that now.

First, we need to get home.

"Our carriages are waiting for us just over that ridge. It will be a long walk, but if we stay together…" His voice trailed off as he looked over his shoulder to find Fewa trembling violently just outside of Ameenah's grasp.

"No. Not here! Not here!" Her voice was frantic as she tried to push Ameenah away from her. "You have to get away from here!"

Fewa turned towards the cliffs that stood behind them and backed away.

"This is the place from which you do not return!" she screamed as Ameenah caught her mother in her arms again.

"Ina, it's all right! We won't let him hurt you. Please."

From the corner of her eyes, Ameenah saw Nasir walk past them towards the cliffs.

"He has already hurt me, child," Fewa replied. "The graves of our ancestors lie open. Can you not hear their screams?"

Suddenly, Ameenah could hear them, the wails of women and men, even animals, pleading for their lives. Ameenah closed her hands over her ears and shut her eyes against the crushing agony, but the sounds gave way to visions of thousands of people being thrown down, down, down into darkness.

Her eyes snapped open at the sensation of her dress whipping in the wind. She looked down to find that the molten gold of her dress had been replaced by an inky darkness that flowed into the night air. She saw fire and death reflected there. Slowly her eyes rose to Nasir as he peered over the cliff's edge, a look of horror twisting his beautiful face.

She knew what he saw. The vision reflected on her dress showed it, too.

"What's wrong?" Kiva asked, drawing nearer to her brother. "What do you see?"

"Death," Fewa replied.

Slowly the others stepped up to the cliff's edge. As if the night no longer had the will to hide its terror, the clouds parted from the second moon. Illuminated by pure moonlight, the dead lay bare by the thousands. Men, women, children, and even strange creatures no one dared to identify lay crushed, burned and crumbled for as far as the eye could see. Some bones were smooth, others still bore their flesh from gaping wounds that would never heal.

Nasir's parents turned away, trembling with their first true understanding of the place to which they had come.

"Who could have done this?" Medi asked, her voice small and full of fear.

"The Hir," Nasir answered. "Maybe even the Hir before him."

"You don't know that," his father replied. "We need time to think. If the Hir is planning war as you say, why would he kill men who could fight for him, even if they would do so only out of fear?"

"Their lives meant nothing to him," Fewa answered. "It is only the weapon he needs."

Nasir stared at Fewa in shock. "What weapon? Do you know where it is?"

"It is not a secret. All of us who come here know what he is looking for, but he won't find it. It is hidden, even from itself."

Nasir strode in front of Fewa and held her by her shoulders.

"What weapon, Ina?! What weapon?"

Fewa stared back at him blankly.

"Nasir," Ameenah urged, pulling her mother from his grasp. "I've tried already. She doesn't know. We need to leave."

Nasir looked at Ameenah for a long moment then stepped back as he tried to shake the immovable fear from his mind.

I can carry my questions until we are safe, he reasoned. *Then we will have time.*

With his family gathered around him, Nasir tried to refocus.

"The carriages are waiting. We'll talk again when it is safe."

They pressed forward with renewed urgency to get as far away from the Hir's grip as possible. But the cliff they were on was steep enough to mask the valley below and the coming of the Hir's forces that were rising up to meet them.

Kiva was the first to see the light from their torches.

"Nasir!" she screamed because there was no point in trying to be quiet anymore.

Understanding came quickly as they immediately backed away from the ridge and came together. Kiva assumed a sparring stance, hands raised, feet staggered apart, ready for battle. Beside her, Nasir drew his sword, as the others folded in around him. To his right, Ameenah stood with her dagger pressed into her right hand and her mother tucked between her and Nasir.

The Hir's men surrounded them easily, but they did not advance. Their orders were simply to make sure none of them escaped until the Hir arrived.

He took his time walking from the back of his army to the front. The torches held by the Hir's men cast menacing shadows across his face and gown, making him appear like a ravaged ghost with angry red marks across his face. Ameenah gasped as she realized his scars were almost healed.

Angered by the notion of any reprieve from the suffering he deserved, Ameenah's eyes fixed on him. She didn't know if they would live or die, but she knew that she would not be captured. Neither she nor her mother would ever see the inside of that cell again.

As she released her fear, fury rose up to take its place, burning through all the painful, empty spaces the man before her had created until her broken heart was melded back together by a fire of pure rage. Suddenly, Ameenah relished the chance to finally face the man who had taken everything from her without pretense.

This will be my reckoning, she thought. *This will be my revenge.*
Ameenah bared her teeth and smiled.

"Ameenah," he began, arms spread wide. "I have been looking for you everywhere. It's rude for a guest to run away from their host."

"Guest? Your men threw me into your chambers. Is it your custom to treat all your guests like prisoners?"

The Hir smiled. "I see you've taken the liberty of finding one of my most treasured guests. Your dressmaker."

"My mother," she spat, trying to push Fewa behind her, but her mother seemed determined to remain by her side. The Hir looked at them with a knowing grin.

"Of course she is. I knew you would recognize her work. She would never weave anything for me, of course, but when I told her it was for you—well, she was so excited. She worked herself nearly to death on it. You know, I've killed so many of your line, at first I wasn't sure who you belonged to. But then I remembered a rumor that Fewa had a daughter who had disappeared. Though my father's men assured me they had killed everyone in your family, something in me never stopped searching for you. Your mother is such a powerful specimen. I had high hopes for you. See?" he said as he began unwrapping the bandages from his finger. "My hand is almost healed because of her."

In the orange light of the torch, his hand looked bloody and raw, but there was no mistaking the outline of two fingers that had not been there mere hours ago.

"Thief!" Ameenah screamed as she looked from the Hir to her mother. "You stole her power for yourself. You stole her from me!" Ameenah felt tears of anger well up within her, but she refused to let them fall.

The Hir continued smugly. "You misunderstand our arrangement. Your mother gives her power to me freely, as is the way of the Amasiti. If she were capable, I would have taken much more from her, but her powers as a Healer have saved me many times. Her willingness to work with me and, of course, the prospect of *you,* are what kept her alive. She has so longed to see you. It's part of what made me believe that somehow you were still alive, and here you are, drawn like a fly into my web."

"You're wrong! I don't have any power, and if I did, I would *never* give it to you!"

"No? Not even for your mother's life? The life of your friends? Dear Opa?"

Ameenah fought to keep her gaze from faltering. She knew that Nasir and Kiva would not give in to his tyranny. They were leaders of the Simbu-Ki. To them, honor and justice were more important than death. It was their creed.

But Opa. Without him here, isn't it my responsibility to fight for his life?

Whatever he wants from you, you must make sure he doesn't get it, Opa had warned her that night by the fire. At the time, Ameenah didn't have an answer for him, but she did now.

I will make sure, Opa, she thought, praying that he and the men they'd hired to protect the farm would be safe, then returned her focus to the threat in front of her.

Out of the corner of her eye, Ameenah saw her mother turn towards her in bewilderment. Slowly, she began running her fingers through Ameenah's hair, fingering her beads and cowrie shells.

"Ina, step back, please," Ameenah begged, trying not to take her eyes off the Hir. Instead, Fewa drew closer.

The Hir looked between them with amusement.

"It's ironic, really. She's been with us for so long. Despite all the things I've made poor Fewa do and witness, it was creating your dress that finally broke her. Perhaps in making the dress for you, she finally realized that all her efforts to hide her last living child from me had failed. The magic in your blood and your craft led me to you anyway."

The belt, Ameenah thought, remembering how Jogg had caressed it. *Of course.*

Suddenly, Fewa stepped in front of her daughter with her arms flailing. "Take me!" she cried. "Take me!"

"No, Ina!" Ameenah grabbed her mother's hand and pulled her back. "Stay with me, Ina! Stay with me as I have stayed with you. Help me fight them!" In desperation, Ameenah clasped her mother's hands together and placed them over the necklace she had worn since she was a child.

The current of energy between them was powerful, sending a shock through both their bodies. For an instant, the jolt created a sphere where only the two of them resided. Somewhere in the blurred background outside their cocoon, Ameenah saw the Hir's eyes widen in alarm.

"Seize them!" he commanded, but the sound of his voice was lost within the sacred space between a mother and her child.

For the first time since she found her, Fewa's eyes met Ameenah's with love and recognition.

"Ameenah?" Fewa gasped, slowly reaching for her child at last. Ameenah covered her mouth and closed her eyes as a sob escaped her lips. Tears of joy ran down her face as she savored the sound of her name on her mother's tongue once more.

"It's me, Ina," Ameenah replied, extending her arms to embrace her. But just as her arms were about to close around her mother, the Hir's guards cut into the bubble of energy that surround them with a tarnished gold sickle and snatched Fewa out of Ameenah's grasp.

"Ina!" Ameenah screamed as the Hir's men held her back. The moment their peace was broken, chaos rushed in to take its place. The Hir's men, who had kept their distance a moment ago, were now upon them.

Nasir lashed out with his sword, slashing through two of the Hir's men before turning his blade in a wide circle, creating a barrier of protection between the onslaught of men and those he sought to protect. But without Kiva to flank his left, it was not enough. As the Hir's men attacked, Jaleen and Medi grabbed their daughter with a tight grip and pulled her furious form to the ground.

"Nasir!" Kiva cried, trying to warn her brother about the men approaching from behind as she writhed underneath her mother's weight. But her parents would not let go—forcing Kiva to watch as her brother was ambushed.

Furious, Kiva could do nothing as her whole family was driven to the ground in seconds. Only Jaleen and Medi could be heard begging for their lives.

The Hir smiled. "Not that one," he said, motioning to the guards who were forcing Ameenah to her knees. "Stand her up. I want her to watch." As if on command, the Hir's guard wrapped his hands around Fewa's throat and began to squeeze.

"Please, NO!" Ameenah begged.

All around her, the people she loved were inches from death, swords at their back. Hands around their necks. And she, as helpless as the child she had been, unable to save her family from harm once more.

Except, she wasn't.

This time she had a choice, and no matter how wrong it was she would make it. She would not lose everything she loved again.

"Take me!" she shouted. "Take me."

Behind her, Ameenah could hear Nasir pleading for her to run. Farther away, Medi cried out for mercy. But Ameenah ignored them all. All her attention was focused on the man to whom her destiny would now belong.

CHAPTER 21

Fewa

"**B**RING HER TO me!" the Hir commanded in a triumphant voice that echoed across the field. "And the necklace. Take it from her now!" Ameenah looked down to find the necklace she had always worn, the necklace her mother had given her, transformed into the smooth black pearlescent stone wrapped in gold that she'd first seen in the forest.

Stunned, Ameenah looked to her mother, but there was only a calm power reflected back at her. Ameenah recognized the look immediately. *This* was her mother.

And then she knew.

Something was happening. Something that Fewa had been planning for a very long time.

A bright light brought Ameenah's guards to a standstill as all eyes turned to Fewa. The soldier who dared to wrap his hands around her neck screamed out in pain as the fire of Fewa's light consumed him.

"Ameenah," Fewa said to her only daughter. "It is time to tell you who you are."

Fewa's light was blinding, sending the men who surrounded her scurrying away or cowering on the ground in terror. The guards who held Ameenah refused to release their grip on her arms even as they shut their eyes and hid behind her to shield themselves from Fewa's burning glow. But in front, Ameenah's eyes were wide with wonder—drawn to the sight of the mother she knew—but had never truly seen until now.

"Release my daughter," Fewa commanded.

The guards that held Ameenah fell to the ground, eyes burning as they skulked away with the rest of the Hir's forces, leaving her alone in a wide-open space.

"Ina!"

"My child." Fewa's feet hovered just above the ground.

"No!" the Hir roared as he grabbed the two guards that remained at his side and thrust them forward. "Do something!"

Feebly, the guards inched forward, shielding their eyes, but as Fewa rose higher and higher into the air, there was nothing they could do.

"So long have I dreamed of this moment, *lived* for the time when you would return to me. There is so much that I would tell you, but we are out of time. My Ascension is the only way that you can be saved, but I have left you all that you need."

Ameenah did not want to understand. All she cared about was keeping the woman who hovered above her close.

"You can't leave," she pleaded through tears of joy and sorrow.

"I have never left you, my child. You are a part of me, a part of *us*. The power within me resides in you. You called it forth, reminding me once more of who I am. Who I will always be. Thank you for saving me."

"But I don't understand, what power?" Ameenah asked, confused. Then she remembered the necklace. Looking down at where it rested on her chest, she remembered what she had seen in the Forbidden Forest.

"Yes, the power within it was hidden, so that the truth of who you are would be hidden as well, but now you must come forth. A great war is coming, my child, and you will be the one to lead them," Fewa explained.

Ameenah shook her head.

"I can't. I don't know how. Please stay with me."

"You are not alone. To lead you must learn to trust again, to become a part of the world that is both seen and unseen. You must call the power forth. I will release it, but to wield it you must know what it is before you can unleash it in others, as you did for me."

"But you are my mother!" How, Ameenah wondered, would she ever have a deeper connection with anyone than what she had with the woman who gave her life?

"You have many mothers. Your family is larger than the one that shares your name. Every person, every plant, every animal is yours, and you are theirs. This was the promise made to me. This is your legacy. That is what it means to be Amasiti."

As Ameenah watched her mother rise over her head and out of reach, her tears became sobs.

"Wait! Don't leave!"

Fewa's expression was sad, but firm. Determined.

"Within the dress, I have woven my memories, everything I know about the powers to which you are entrusted, but you will learn more, *be* more than I ever could. You will forge a new path with new allies to travel with you."

Underneath the fullness of her mother's voice, Ameenah felt the ground tremble as a second wave of the Hir's army charged towards them. Before her eyes, her mother's light was fading.

Though the danger was imminent, Ameenah could not find it within her to care.

"Ina!"

Behind her, Nasir readied himself for a new attack while Kiva warned her parents from trying to keep her from the battle again.

But all Ameenah could feel was the light, the warmth that was her mother slipping away into darkness.

"Please," she whispered, collapsing to her knees.

"Rise!" her mother commanded in a voice that rumbled through the air into the deepest spaces of her being, the force of it shaking away her grief. Ameenah stumbled back to her feet. "The Amasiti do not kneel."

But how do I defeat them? Ameenah asked, reaching out to her mother with her mind.

"The power you have given me—I give back to you."

Fewa extended her hand, sending a bolt of lightning through Ameenah's body that knocked her backward and into the air. Weightless, she hovered, spinning slowly in a timeless space where only their connection existed.

They wait for you, Ameenah. Call them! Her mother's voice rippled through her, as loud as a clap of thunder and as profound as a whisper. *You are their chosen,* she said. *Call and they will come.*

The sound of wolves howling vibrated through her, from the distant plains or from her own throat—she did not know. Power surged through her like wildfire, awakening and transforming the dress until it was alive. Shifting from molten gold into tiny threads of light that dissolved into her very skin, extending from her body in every direction, from limb to limb. Flashes of memories, scenes from a life she never lived came crashing into her consciousness: The rhythm of women dancing in tandem with the light of the universe at their fingertips. The wounded whimper of a mother as all but one of her pups were slaughtered. Sri looking back at her from the forest with scorn and wonder in his eyes. And a glittering island receding from the shore into the depths of the sea.

A strange new presence emerged within her, one with a voice of thunder and a ravenous instinct to tear apart anything that stood in its way. It needed none of her reason as it swelled, taking over her mind and transforming her body.

Around her the fibers of the dress burned into her skin until they were one. She landed on all four feet with a snarl that could be heard over the echo of gasps around her. Ameenah looked at the night sky with new eyes to find the fading vision of her mother, tears in her eyes, surrounded by the spirit faces of hundreds of women she did not know, but felt all the same.

The Wolf Queen, Praise the Mother, they whispered in awe before fading away completely.

Ameenah answered with a howl that echoed through the night and was answered by a force more powerful than any she had ever known.

CHAPTER 22

A New Road

"KILL IT! KILL that thing!" the Hir shouted as Ameenah turned to face her prey.

Her body felt enormous as her head moved from side to side, snarling at the Hir and the men who dared to creep towards her with swords drawn. The smell of their fear made her rake her hands and feet into the ground, ready to tear, ready to bite. The sensation was feral, but calming, too, as if she had evolved past all her fears, leaving only the certainty of what must be done before her. It was only what she saw in Nasir's face, eyes wide with uncertain fear and a sadness she could not understand, that made her pause long enough to look down.

To her utter shock, she was covered in burnished gold fur, with strong and lean limbs. They belonged to an animal. They belonged to a wolf. The sight should have frightened her, but somehow it did not. Though Ameenah had no recollection of how she came to be this way, nothing in her felt unnatural.

To the contrary, as she scraped her large paws against the ground and bared her teeth to the men who were running up the hill behind Nasir, Ameenah had never been surer that she was exactly what and who she was meant to be.

Do not be afraid, she tried to say, but her voice came out as a mournful howl that only seemed to unnerve him more. Ameenah growled in frustration as Nasir backed away from the ferocity in her stance.

Ameenah realized then that the emotion between them was too complex for the simplicity of her thoughts. Right now, she was a wolf, and that was all she had time to be. Without another thought, Ameenah leapt up, over Nasir's shoulder and crashed down upon the two men Nasir had not noticed at his back. With an efficiency she could immediately appreciate, Ameenah ripped through them with a snap of her jaw, one by one. Their blood was warm and delicious as it slid down her throat.

"Attack!" the Hir yelled as he retreated farther and farther behind his own soldiers, but they did not move. His army had heard the call of the wolves. Their howls echoed from every corner of the vast forest that defined the borders of Mera Meja, making it impossible to know from which direction their attack would come.

The screaming began at the palace gates as the Hir's guests fled from the first pack of wolves bursting into the courtyard, rushing towards the cliffs to answer Ameenah's call. But the second and third packs were much closer, breaking through the trees and onto the palace grounds. Ameenah felt their heartbeats racing through her as if they were her own, and the weight of their claws as they tore through the cursed land the Hir had wrought.

After recovering from the initial shock of Ameenah's transformation, Nasir and Kiva used the soldiers' hesitation to regain the upper hand and extinguish any man who dared to come within striking distance. But they did not run. Instead, they formed a tight flank around Nasir's parents and maintained a healthy distance from the Hir's men to distinguish themselves. When the wolves came, Nasir and Kiva did not want to be in their path.

But Ameenah would not wait.

With the pulse of the wolves' collective fury coursing through her veins, she attacked. Her first move was to bite the hand that held the sword closest to her. Her strong jaws pulled the soldier down easily. Once the man was on the ground, she launched herself at another who tried to close in on Nasir's parents.

From behind her line of assault, Kiva and Nasir watched in awe as the wolf packs converged. Without any discernable signal, a small group of wolves broke away from the pack, surrounding their family in an impenetrable cocoon while the larger group rushed forward to face their enemies as one force. Those of the Hir's men who did not have the sense to flee died in a terrifying display of power and precision. Afterwards, the wolves ran down the rest of the Hir's infantry.

After tearing through the Hir's first line of men, Ameenah searched for the Hir himself, but in the pit of her stomach, she already knew she would not find him among the fallen or even those still fleeing. In her mind, she could almost see him, cowering behind the barred gates and high walls of his palace. Briefly she considered seeking him out, to finally end his legacy of cruelty.

All around her, the wolves that were not in pursuit of the Hir's men hovered, sensing the moment of her decision, waiting for her command.

How many lives would we lose?

Too many, she decided.

The wolves' advantage, *her* advantage, lay in the field. Against the palace gates, there would be no victory… today.

Ameenah turned her head to the precipice on her right and inhaled the stench of the dead, some as recent as last week, others from hundreds of years ago.

Even in wolf form, she understood that killing one man would not stop a plot that was hundreds of years old.

There is never just one road, just one way, just one person. This is not how problems start and it is never how they end.

Though her memory of Opa's words was clouded, she felt their meaning as clearly as the wind against her fur. With a loud snap of her jaw, she turned away.

To defeat the people behind all that happened and all that was to come, she would need to understand what had led them to this place and why. She would also need an army made of more than just wolves.

A great war, her mother had called it.

And a great war it will be.

With a howl, Ameenah turned, leading her pack towards the carriages that Nasir had secured for their escape.

Without the rush of battle to focus her, a deeper awareness expanded in her mind. Ameenah watched Nasir as he escorted his parents and sister to one carriage, then turned to face her. Though his face was hard, unreadable, it was the smell of his fear that finally stopped Ameenah in her tracks.

She cocked her head to one side as the unthinkable came into focus once more.

He is afraid of me. It was more a thought than a feeling, but it broke her heart just the same.

Should he be?

Ameenah took a step back as she realized she wasn't entirely sure of the answer.

Are we safe?

Once again, she was acutely aware of what she was and who she wasn't.

With a low howl, Ameenah sent her pack away, thanking them for their help and warning them to be cautious on the way home. At the edge of the forest, a lone wolf with tawny hair—*her* wolf—waited for her.

When the space between them was quiet once more, Ameenah turned towards Nasir.

Now there is only one of us for him to fear, she thought.

Slowly, Nasir closed the door to his family carriage and walked to his own. Knowing she could not speak to him in any language he could fathom, he used none as he opened the door and waited, wondering if she could or would return to herself again.

Ameenah's approach was slow. As she closed the distance between them, she took her time listening to his heartbeat and smelling the waning intensity of his fear. On all fours, she reached his chest easily. If she raised onto her hind legs, she would tower over him by at least two feet.

All her life, he'd been careful with her; now she would try to do the same. When Nasir was steady enough to hold his ground, Ameenah tried to comfort him the only way she knew how. Gently, she pressed her head against his chest, hearing his sadness, smelling his fear, then stepped back.

His expression as she moved away from him was a tortured mix of agony and disbelief, but when Ameenah tried to say she was sorry, the sound that came out was more of a whine. Nasir blinked at her, mouth agape without a single word worth saying.

With no answers for the questions behind his eyes, Ameenah turned away. Her mind was still guided by instinct and the astonishing newness of her transformation. She could offer him no more. So she ran, racing toward her pack, and hoping he would follow.

OTHER BOOKS BY

Cerece Rennie Murphy

SCIENCE FICTION

Order of the Seers (Book I)
Order of the Seers: The Red Order (Book II)
Order of the Seers: The Last Seer (Book III)

EARLY READER CHAPTER BOOKS
WWW.THEELLISSERIES.COM
Ellis and The Magic Mirror
Ellis and The Hidden Cave
Ellis and The Cloud Kingdom (coming soon!)

HISTORICAL ROMANCE/SCI-FI

To Find You

SIGN-UP FOR EXCLUSIVES, NEWS UPDATES AND MORE AT
WWW.CERECERENNIEMURPHY.COM

ABOUT

Cerece Rennie Murphy

NATIONAL BESTSELLING AND award-winning author Cerece Rennie Murphy fell in love with writing and science fiction at an early age. It's a love affair that has grown ever since. In 2012, Mrs. Murphy published the first book in what would become the Order of the Seers sci-fi trilogy. Mrs. Murphy has since published nine books and short stories, including her latest release and first fantasy series, The Wolf Queen.

Mrs. Murphy and her son are also working on completing Ellis and The Cloud Kingdom, the 3rd book in the Ellis and the Magic Mirror early reader children's book series. They hope to release Ellis and the Cloud Kingdom in late 2018.

Mrs. Murphy lives and writes in her hometown of Washington, DC with her husband, two children and the family dog, Yoda. To learn more about the author and her upcoming projects, please visit her website at

WWW.CERECERENNIEMURPHY.COM